THE ADVENTURE OF THE CHRISTMAS CRACKER

and other short stories

Harriet Loveday

Harriet Loveday Romance

First published in Great Britain in 2021 by: Harriet Loveday Romance and KDP

ISBN-13: 978-1-7398975-1-2

Book production: Harriet Loveday Romance
Cover design: Harriet Loveday Romance
Cover image: Unsplash, Joanna Kosinska
Copy-editing/proofreading: Harriet Loveday Romance

For

Mum, Gran, Theresa, Gill and Daphne

#womensupportingwomen

CONTENTS

PREFACE

My mum grew up in the West Country. She once told me an anecdote of a lady who lived in her village, who had five sons, all from different fathers. They lived in a council house with wallpaper peeling off the walls, and they struggled for enough food to eat and heating to keep warm. But. She loved her sons and her sons adored her. They were a family. The lady was loved and well looked after in her later years by her sons. I believe love is at the root of everything. This story has always stuck with me and was my inspiration for *The Other Side of the (Christmas Train) Tracks.*

This anthology of Christmas-themed, short stories centres around love. Some of the stories are amusing, some are heart-warming, a couple are thought-provoking. So put your feet up, grab a hot chocolate, tea or coffee, and let me transport you to a world of my imagination.

HL x (December 2021)

1. MARY'S CHRISTMAS CAROL

Old Mary Wise shuffled along the cobbled street, in the cold and the dark, towards the cathedral. The wind seemed particularly bitter tonight, and she pulled her coat a little tighter round her. The cathedral glowed ahead of her like a beacon of light and happiness. Just like a moth, she fluttered her way towards it.

Mary was going to see her great-grandson perform. She hadn't checked her hair; it was probably wild, grey and frizzy, and her clothes were old fashioned and worn, but none of that mattered. She longed to hear his beautiful voice rise with the other choristers; singing festive Christmas carols and practising for the December services.

Mary shuffled into the entrance. It wasn't exactly warm inside the cathedral, but without the wind it was much better. She was glad of her coat. Stepping silently down the aisle, she slid into a pew three rows back from her great-grandson. The man in the pew in front turned around to look at her, and she smiled back, but he just shook his head and returned his attention to the singing children. “People are definitely ruder these days.” she thought to herself.

In-between carols Mary waved to her great-grandson Luca, and he waved back. Her heart burst with pride. Such a lovely little boy. He needed a good father influence.

Mary’s heart wept for her pretty granddaughter Estelle. It was hard for Estelle as a single mother. But understandably, Estelle had lost her trust of men, and she was trying to do it all alone. All of it. Work, parenting for two, DIY, decisions. Estelle had little emotional support as her parents (Mary’s son and daughter-in-law) lived in Spain. Although Estelle's parents tried to help out financially when she was in a jam (a job that should have sat with the father) they couldn’t provide the emotional support she needed. Most of the time they weren’t even aware, as Estelle battled on alone, never complaining, never asking. Trying to do it all. “My little Golden Girl.” Mary thought, with a tear in her eye.

The carols sung by the choristers were enchanting. A little slice of heaven in this ancient, well-lit cathedral, on a dark December evening. Then, all too soon, it was over. The children were grabbing their coats and putting on their mittens.

Mary looked around for her granddaughter, she felt a little panicked for her great-grandson. “Where is she?” she thought to herself. People started leaving the cathedral. A cold blast of air rushed in. Mary turned towards the back entrance, "Ahh! There." At the back of the cathedral, rushing up the aisle, in the same coat that she'd worn for the last five years - yet as beautiful as ever, was Estelle. Mary struggled to get up and wave to her, but Estelle didn't see her and rushed past. Mary wanted to say something, but she was afraid of making a fuss.

In Estelle's haste to get to Luca she accidentally bumped into one of the other children's fathers. Nearly knocking herself to the floor the man quickly managed to grab Estelle's arm and right her.

'Oh, my fault!' Estelle exclaimed.

'Not at all, the fault's all mine.' He was tall and good-looking, with light-grey eyes. Estelle and the man smiled briefly at each other before she came to her senses and rushed off.

"Humm." Mary thought to herself, "Now that's interesting."

'Luca? Good you're ready.' Estelle gasped to refill her lungs with air. Leaning down she pulled his scarf a little tighter. 'We've got to rush for the bus.'

'But Mum . . .' Luca pointed at Mary, who was holding tightly to the pews, as she stood with a little wobble and a sway.

'Come on darling.'

'But Mum . . .'

'Not now.'

Estelle dragged Luca back down the aisle as he turned his head back towards Mary and smiled.

Mary smiled back. "Dear boy." she thought.

Mary momentarily considered trying to follow them back. She had done so a few times. But there was something wrong with Estelle's doorbell; no matter how many times she rang, Estelle never came to answer. Mary turned her attention to the tall, handsome gentleman with the light-grey eyes. She watched him tickle his son on the back of his head as they walked away from her to exit the cathedral. She hadn't noticed a wedding ring. Pulling her coat a little tighter round her, Mary decided she would investigate. No harm in it. As quickly as she could she shuffled off down the aisle in pursuit of the man and the boy.

* * *

The next Tuesday old Mary Wise shuffled along the same, familiar, cobbled street, towards the cathedral. She was a little earlier than usual this evening. She had a plan.

Estelle was already seated in a pew at the front, quite close to the aisle. Estelle wasn't running errands today and was taking a moment to enjoy listening to her son. She kept these golden memories safe in her heart. Childhood and life move by so quickly, she wanted to cherish and enjoy these moments when she could.

Mary smiled. Estelle and Luca shared such a close bond. It was beautiful to anyone who could *see*. Mary scanned the cathedral. The man with the lovely grey eyes wasn't here yet. The choristers were only just starting to assemble.

A lady rudely bumped into Mary. Mary turned around in surprise, but the lady didn't even apologise, she just carried on up the aisle with her little girl, ready for the evening's choir practice. The problem with being a little old lady is that people really don't notice you all that much. However, Mary's plan was to use that to her advantage tonight.

Mary shuffled up the aisle towards the choir. Luca looked up and saw her. Giving her a big smile, he waved. Mary waved back. Estelle turned around to see whom he was waving to, but looked straight past Mary without a flicker of recognition. Mary consoled herself that her appearance was a little bedraggled; she should have combed her hair. Perhaps Estelle was embarrassed to be associated with her? She wasn't offended. All of Mary's memories of afternoons spent reading to the pretty, little, golden-haired girl came flooding back to her. She fondly remembered making crazy cake recipes, with strange ingredients such as: rice, cucumber and flour, like some kind of *George's Marvellous Medicine* cake. Or when Mary had a new litter of kittens and Estelle would sit on the kitchen chair by the stove, her skinny legs swinging in the air, stroking a little bundle of fluff. Yes, their love and memories were much deeper than a missed glance now and again. Her beautiful Golden Girl.

Mary sat a couple of pews back from Estelle, next to the aisle. She lay in wait for the handsome gentleman to arrive. She didn't have to wait long. A few more children and parents arrived, then . . . there he was, with his son. His son rushed ahead of his him as he was one of the last children to arrive. The man walked up the aisle behind him, looking for an empty pew to perch on. He drew level with Mary, and Mary, unobserved, stuck out her foot.

The man went flying and landed somewhere near Estelle's feet.

'Oh!' an audible cry rose from the people present. Some tried to rush to help him. Estelle had her hand over her mouth and bent down to help him up. But, predictably, flushed with embarrassment, he pushed himself up to his feet as quickly as he could, assured everyone he was fine, looked behind in a puzzled manner, and, not noticing Mary, sat down hastily next to Estelle.

Mary smiled. She knew it was a little naughty. But there were advantages to being a little old lady that nobody notices.

* * *

It was just as Mary had planned. The natural chemistry between Estelle and the man ignited. She could see them whispering between carols and she even thought she heard Estelle giggle at one point. At the end of the practice Mary hastily got to her feet to shuffle a little nearer.

'Adam.' Mary heard the man re-introduce himself as he shook Estelle's hand. 'And this is my son Robert.'

Estelle beamed at Robert, as he and Luca arrived at the same time to the pew where their parents had been talking.

'My son is Luca.' said Estelle, indicating to Luca, who gravitated towards his mum with a surprised look.

Adam smiled at Luca. Luca and Robert exchanged glances. Adam gulped and said, 'Look, I know this is a little untoward, and I don't want you to think anything of it. But would you like to go for a coffee sometime?'

Four pairs of expectant eyes turned to Estelle.

'Why, why, I'd love to.' she replied.

'Oh. Well, that's great. Umm. Look, here's my number.' Adam reached into his pocket and pulled out a business card. 'You know who I am now too. Not a stalker! But seriously, this bottom one is my personal mobile. Text me when you're free this week.'

Estelle accepted the card and thanked him. Then she watched Adam and Robert walk down the aisle and exit the cathedral. She held the card in her hand thoughtfully, as Luca looked up to her and said, 'He seems really nice Mum.'

'Oh Luca.' Estelle smiled and placed the card on the seat of the pew, before pulling on her gloves. 'The only nice men I know are you, my dad and my grandfather. There are a lot of *not* nice men out there.' Estelle tried to stroke away the confusion from her son's face. 'Come on. We're going to be late for the bus.'

Luca tried to turn around to Mary to say goodbye, but his mum was already pulling him down the aisle. All he managed was a smile and Mary smiled back, but her mind was whizzing. What should she do? Mary turned to the rejected business card left on the seat of the pew, and grabbing it, rushed as fast as she could after them. She had a plan.

* * *

The children from next door kicked the football at the front door of Estelle's small, semi-detached house again.

'Right!' Estelle said, putting her dinner tray down and getting up off the sofa. She went to the front door and opened it angrily. Only to be greeted by a cold wind and a dark evening. The children had obviously heard her coming. Crossly she closed the door and put the safety chain on. Damn kids. Estelle came back into the living room and plopped down on the sofa next to Luca, making his tray wobble. She grabbed her tray of egg and chips, and speared a chip as she said, 'Next time I'm going to catch one of those kids.'

'What kids?' said Luca.

'The ones with the football. Just now.' She looked at Luca as if he was deaf.

'That's not kids.' said Luca confidently. 'That's

Old Granny Mary. She wants to come in.'

Estelle sat frozen with a chip mid-delivery. It was as if someone had just given her a very cold, unexpected, electric shock. 'I'm sorry?' she finally managed.

Luca continued mid-mouthful, 'Old Granny Mary. She wants to come in. But you haven't invited her, so she can't.'

Estelle put down her fork and turned with amazement to her son. Sure, she'd talked about her granny a few times to him. But not often, not recently. Estelle continued in a factual voice, 'Luca. Granny Mary died ten years ago.'

'I know.' said Luca. He was starting to feel a bit annoyed. Adults never seemed to listen or *see*.

'Then how can she be outside?'

'Because she wants to speak to you. Only you won't let her in.'

Estelle was stupefied. Her son's rational logic flew in the face of reality. The sane part of her would have told him to stop being ridiculous and to stop making up stories, except for one thing. Love. Estelle had loved her Granny Mary so much; they'd had such a lovely connection. Granny Mary had always had time for Estelle, listening to her and teaching her things. She'd called Estelle her "Golden Girl". Estelle would happily give up any credibility or semblance of normality if it meant she could have a hug from her granny again, if she could hear her voice one last time, if she could be around her warmth and cheerfulness. Her heart longed to see her just once more.

'Where is she?' Estelle asked.

'She's at the door. She's cold. I think you should let her in.'

Estelle and Luca abandoned the last of their egg and chips, as Estelle slowly made her way to the front door. Opening it cautiously, she said in an uncertain voice, 'Granny? Is it you? Granny? Please come in.'

Oh! It had been so cold out there. Mary was glad to enter the warmth of the house. She smiled at Luca and gently kissed his forehead as she made her way into the small, cosy living room and sat down on the armchair near the gas fire.

Estelle locked the front door. Then she and Luca went into the living room and sat down on the sofa.

'Where's Granny?' Estelle asked her son.

'She's sitting in the armchair near the fire.' he said. Estelle turned to look right through Mary.

"Always the same." Mary thought. But it was ok. She was used to it. Estelle didn't mean to be rude, but it was just as Luca often thought, "Some people don't *see*."

Mary spoke to Luca, "Your mum needs to call the nice man from the cathedral."

Luca turned to his mum, 'Granny Mary says you have to call the nice man from the cathedral. Robert's dad.' he added.

'Well, I can't.' Estelle replied to thin air. 'I don't have his number.'

Mary continued, "Tell your mum the number is in her coat pocket."

Luca relayed, 'Granny Mary said it's in your coat pocket.'

'But it can't be, because I left the card on the pew . . .' Estelle got up to go to the coats hall. She came back with an amazed look on her face, holding the little business card. 'It's right here.' she said.

'We told you.' replied Luca.

Mary wiggled her bottom and got cosy by the fire. For once it was nice to be warm. For once it was nice to be seen – sort of.

Estelle turned to her son. She gulped for the right words, then said quietly, 'Could you tell Granny thank you. I'll call him. Could you tell her I love her very much and I miss her. And that's she's more than welcome to stay as long as she likes.'

Luca listened for a moment, then replied to his mother, 'She said thank you, she'd like to stay for a while, and that she loves you too. She said you're her . . . "Golden Girl"?'

Hot tears flooded down Estelle's face as she nodded with recognition at her granny's pet name for her. A name that she hadn't heard for many years.

* * *

The next Tuesday Mary watched from her place in the pew, as the man with the light-grey eyes,

Adam, gravitated towards Estelle, who was seated two rows back from the choir. He and Estelle exchanged warm smiles, and Estelle shuffled along the pew to make room for him next to her.

Mary watched her beautiful Golden Girl, with tears in her eyes. Yes, an architect, that would do quite nicely. Luca smiled and waved at Mary from the choir and Mary waved back. Luca needed a *good* father influence. Yes, this young man Adam would do very nicely. Mary smiled to herself. She was feeling rather content. And it was nearly Christmas. She loved Christmas.

'Ahem.' a gentleman coughed politely next to Mary and motioned to the seat next to her along the pew.

Mary was surprised. She was so used to people not noticing her, that she'd almost forgotten her social graces. She smoothed her hair back as she twisted her knees round to let the man past her, on into the pew.

He wore a smart grey coat and had a small posy of pink Michaelmas flowers, held in a small, sliver nosegay on his coat lapel. His face was non-descript; a little wrinkly, an average face, slightly tanned; with two deep-set, kind, blue eyes. He had a gentle way about him.

'Cold evening.' he said in a conversational tone to Mary.

Mary smiled back as a draft wiggled around her legs. 'Yes, it is!' she confirmed brightly. Mary was always good with people. Everyone liked her.

'Is that your granddaughter?' the man continued, pointing to Estelle a couple of rows ahead.

'Yes. Yes, it is. Beautiful girl. She's had a hard time, and she deserves so much, but I think the tide is about to turn for her. I think she deserves something good in her life. Don't you?' she replied, turning around to look at the man.

He smiled as he said, 'Yes. Yes, I do.' He pointed again, 'And that is your great-grandson Luca?'

'Yes.' Mary beamed. 'He's a lovely boy.'

'Very sensitive. A treasure.' the man agreed. 'His lesson will be to learn to discern whom to give his empathy to, and who is trying to take advantage of him.' he smiled in a pleasant manner.

Mary turned to the stranger with a worried look on her face. The stranger laid a reassuring hand on her arm. 'Don't worry, it will be difficult, but he has a good heart, he will succeed.' He paused and offered Mary his hand, 'I'm so sorry, I didn't introduce myself. My name is Michael.'

Mary took his hand and shook it. Candidly she replied, 'It's my time, isn't it?'

'Yes,' Michael calmly responded, 'it's your time.'

'How long have I got before we have to go?' she looked desperately towards her granddaughter and great-grandson. Estelle and Adam's heads were locked together in whispers as they both watched their sons perform. Luca was singing with the other children in the choir. He looked so young and beautiful. Mary couldn't bear to know he would have hard lessons to learn in the world.

She wanted to be here to protect him from it. She wanted to stay.

Michael replied in an easy manner, 'Well, I'm very busy, but time is such a relative thing. Would the end of the choir practice be ok?'

Mary nodded gratefully as little tears sprang to her eyes, knowing this would be the last time.

Michael offered her a tissue as he consoled her, 'They will only be as far away as the horizon, just because we can't see over the horizon doesn't mean our hearts stop loving.' He placed his hand on her arm again, as he gently reminded her, 'Remember, love is infinite, it is beyond time.' And through her hot tears Mary nodded, as she watched her family with loving eyes. Her granddaughter and the man with the beautiful, light-grey eyes moved closer together on the bench, Mary had a good feeling about them. She turned her gaze back to Luca, stood amongst his friends, singing. Listening for the last time, she was quite sure that she'd never heard anything so beautiful in her life.

2. THE ADVENTURE OF THE CHRISTMAS CRACKER

Jarrod cleared his throat. 'I would be very grateful sir, if you would allow me to propose to your daughter.' Beads of sweat ran down the back of his neck and under the collar of his crisp, blue shirt. He placed his hands calmly on his knees and tried to look respectable and worthy.

Bill Rich sized up his daughter's boyfriend. Jarrod had neatly cut, brown hair and an athletic physique. He was a lovely guy, a bit dopey now and then, but a good, honest man with a kind heart. And he loved Bill's daughter. Bill had been dreading this day, and yet, for Vicky his daughter, he had been wanting it too. He watched young Jarrod Worthy squirm and waited a few seconds longer before replying.

'I'd be delighted to call you my son-in-law. You have my blessing.'

Jarrod looked for a second as if he was about to faint. Instead, the two men embraced and clapped each other on the back. Then looking away, they both tried to wipe a little tear from their eyes without the other noticing and agreed on a drink of scotch to celebrate.

Irene Rich sat in her immaculate kitchen, idly turning the pages of her home magazine with her perfectly manicured hands. She had a good idea why Jarrod had wanted to visit today, in secret, and without Vicky. From the sounds of self-congratulations in the study, she also had a pretty good idea that she was right. She closed her magazine and reaching for her expensive handbag pulled out a bridal magazine. What were the latest mother of the bride fashions these days?

Bill and Jarrod eventually surfaced from the study, two drinks later, flushed and happy with themselves. Irene hastily stowed her magazine away, and smiled in a composed, calm manner.

'Darling,' Bill said, 'I'd like to introduce you to our new son-in-law!' and in so doing slapped Jarrod good naturedly on the back.

Irene did a wonderful job of acting surprised. Young Jarrod was covered in kisses and everyone congratulated each other.

'We have also decided,' Bill announced, 'how the proposal should be done.'

"Uh-oh," thought Irene, "the first fly in the ointment."

Jarrod and Bill beamed as Jarrod blurted out, 'I'm going to propose at the family Christmas lunch, with the engagement ring inside a Christmas cracker!'

Irene smiled happily. She could see this wasn't going to go to plan already.

* * *

Vicky and Jarrod pulled up at her parent's house in their old estate car. The presents were spilling out of reusable supermarket bags in the boot. They were late as Jarrod had taken two wrong turns. Vicky was annoyed, and angrily flicked open the visor mirror to check to see if her straight, brown hair was still straight, and her makeup was still looking fresh. Two pretty blue eyes stared back at her. It wasn't as if Jarrod hadn't driven to her parent's house before. They were almost certainly the last to arrive, she thought, as they struggled to find a spot on the driveway.

They weren't the last to arrive, but it was going to be a busy house this year. Invited - alongside Vicky and Jarrod, and her parents Bill and Irene - would be her crazy Aunt Alice (always getting bailed out by Vicky's parents) and her new boyfriend Stephano, who was possibly as equally crazy as Aunt Alice. They would all find out soon, as this was the first opportunity for the family to meet Stephano. Also in attendance were Vicky's two older brothers, their glamorous wives, and one daughter apiece. Both Vicky's brothers had done well; one worked in investment banking and the other was a lawyer working for a large, multinational company. Then there would be Jenny, her mum's best friend from school. Jenny had been widowed for nearly ten years now. Vicky's parents clearly had a plan, as the final invite to lunch was one of her dad's golfing buddies, Charles. He, similarly, had been widowed for at least three years and wasn't coping well on his own.

Vicky didn't mind, she liked large gatherings, and with her family it came with the territory. Her mum, Irene, was an expert in passing off supermarket gourmet as home cooking. Vicky had no doubt that the dining room table had been covered with the old, large, MDF board, hidden by a crisp, white, cotton tablecloth, and adorned with Christmas candles. Her family were good at putting on an acceptable exterior. It was likely to be a very pleasant lunch, if her aunt's new boyfriend was the right side of sane.

Jarrod fussed about the parking. Rather than start an argument or feel frustrated with him, Vicky decided to go on in. Jarrod thought that was an excellent idea and seemed delighted to be carrying in all the presents.

Vicky fought with her scarf and gloves in the hallway. Her parents were extra enthusiastic to see her. Once Vicky had fussed over her nieces, she settled down, drink in hand, to chat with her sisters-in-law. Slowly unwinding from the stressful car journey, Vicky started to feel an awful lot better. Her Aunt Alice and Stephano hadn't arrived yet. Her brothers were playing pool downstairs in the basement. In the hall she could hear her dad and Jarrod sorting out the presents. Vicky wandered out to the hall to offer a hand. She was feeling guilty about being cross at Jarrod. He really was a dear.

'Can I help?' Vicky asked.

Her dad replied, 'Absolutely not sweetheart, Jarrod and I have everything under control. As long as you don't mind the order for the presents under the tree?'

'Not at all!' Vicky replied. 'Ok, perhaps I'd better help Mum in the kitchen.'

Her dad winked at her, 'I think she's opened most of the packets this morning.'

Vicky smiled at the family joke. Then she leant over Jarrod, who was fishing through the bags, and said, 'Thanks love, I really appreciate all that you do.'

Jarrod looked deeply into her blue eyes and replied, 'I know you do.'

Vicky felt all tingly. Then she caught her dad looking at them and she felt awkward. 'I'll go help Mum!' she said and wandered off.

'Mum?' Vicky said, peering round the kitchen door. She was never quite sure if her mum wanted her under her feet or not. This time apparently not.

'Oh I'm glad you're here love,' her mum replied, 'I need some holly from the end of the garden.'

'Really?'

'Yes.'

'But it's cold and snowy out there.'

Her mum gave her a hard stare. 'Look Vicky, everyone is doing their bit, I think you should help too.' Vicky felt guilty. Fair enough. Her mum handed her a carrier bag, secateurs and a pair of gardening gloves. 'Fill this if you would.'

Vicky argued back, 'That's a lot of holly. How big is the pudding?'

'I want some for the table decorations too.'

'Really?'

'I've asked you once Vicky.'

Again, the hard stare. Vicky felt fourteen again. 'Ok Mum.' She sighed as she placed her champagne flute on the worktop and went to get toggled up.

* * *

A box of unicorn-coloured Christmas crackers sat open on the table in front of them.

'Unicorns?' Bill said with bemusement.

'I needed the colours.' Irene defended herself. 'Ok.' she continued, whispering in a loud voice, and holding aloft *the* cracker to Jarrod and Bill, 'There will only be one pink cracker on the table. This one has the ring. I have removed the other two pink crackers, so there is no chance they can get confused. Jarrod, you are one side of Vicky, and Bill you are on the other side, so make sure she will definitely get the ring when the crackers are pulled. We'll open the crackers as soon as we have starters. Everyone knows what they're going to do?' Bill looked wise and smug. Jarrod looked petrified. Both nodded.

Bill hugged his wife and said, 'Don't worry dear, it's going to be fine.'

Irene really wished she could believe him. But somewhere, in the deep, hungry, grumblings of her tummy, she had a feeling something was about to go very wrong.

* * *

Once Vicky's brothers had surfaced from their pool match downstairs, and her aunt and aunt's boyfriend had arrived, then things started to feel very busy. Every room had people in it, and her nieces were as high as kites with the attention. The other person who appeared to be getting a lot of attention was Stephano.

Far from the disasters or dependent victims her aunt usually went for, Stephano was a real catch. He had sun-kissed, Mediterranean skin; dark-brown eyes; a voice dipped in honey, and he seemed to be completely enamoured with Aunt Alice. Palpable surprise rippled through the family. Irene almost blushed when Stephano offered to help her with the *hors d'oeuvres*.

Irene's school friend Jenny arrived next. She seemed a little flustered and nervous. Probably not helped by the fact that Irene whisked her off to put some red lipstick on her, to "give her a Christmas pick-me-up". Jenny looked very uncomfortable when she next came downstairs. Everyone tried to reassure her that she looked great.

Finally, the doorbell rang for the last guest, Charles, Bill's golfing buddy. He'd obviously been primed as he arrived smelling of a strong, spicy aftershave.

Vicky started to feel a little dazed by all the comings and goings, so she disappeared to the cool dining room for five minutes, before everyone sat down to lunch.

As she closed the door, she heard giggling from under the huge, square, MDF Christmas table, which was laid for fourteen. Suspiciously she raised the cloth to find her nieces and a pile of unicorn crackers under the table. They'd opened four already.

'Girls!' Vicky cried. 'What are you doing?'

They looked guilty and said almost simultaneously, 'Sorry Auntie Vicky.'

'Those crackers are for lunch. How many have you opened?'

'Four.' said Grace.

'Come on, out from under the table, let's put them back.'

The girls scrambled out with their loot, and reluctantly started distributing the crackers back round the table. Vicky went to the cupboard to replace the missing ones. She found the empty boxes in the cupboard but only two spare crackers. "That's strange," she said to herself, "three packs of six, that's eighteen in total, if there are fourteen people to lunch, and two crackers here, then there must be another two crackers somewhere?" Vicky started opening drawers and peering in the sideboard cupboards.

'Ah!' she said, as she pulled out two pink crackers from the back of a drawer, and placed one on her side plate, next to her name card. A little pink unicorn covered in festive holly danced happily over it. "Why on earth has Mum got these ridiculous crackers?" she thought. Shrugging, Vicky placed the other pink cracker on the empty side plate for Jenny's setting. She grabbed her champagne flute and ushered the girls out of the dining room, before they did anymore damage.

* * *

'Bong, bong, bong!' The girls held up the novelty gong and went from room to room, rounding everyone up.

'Lunch! Lunch!' the girls sang out.

Everyone was more than ready to eat and hungrily left for the dining room. Vicky settled herself in-between her dad and Jarrod. Jarrod looked completely white, almost as if he was about to be sick.

'You ok love?' she asked, giving his shoulder a squeeze.

He looked back at her with devotion. 'Yes.' he squeaked.

'You don't seem it. Do you want some fresh air?

No one will miss you.'

He barely managed a "No." before Vicky's dad stood up to welcome everyone.

'Dear friends and family . . .' Bill announced, looking around and smiling broadly.

Vicky gave Jarrod a reassuring hug, as he insisted he was fine.

Vicky's dad continued . . . 'Finally, and most importantly,' he paused for emphasis, 'it is time to pull the traditional Christmas cracker!' he finished proudly, sitting back down with his Christmas cracker held firmly in his hand.

There was a little buzz of excitement as everyone reached for their cracker and tried to work out who to pull it with.

Irene looked on with glee as Vicky picked up her pink cracker. Crossing hands with Jarrod's green cracker they pulled hard and . . . out popped a little pink unicorn, a purple paper hat and a joke. Jarrod's face froze as Vicky balanced the unicorn carefully on her dessert spoon.

Like a train crash in slow motion everyone turned to stare, as Vicky's Aunt Alice squealed, 'It's a ring! It's a beautiful diamond ring!'

There, in Aunt Alice's prawn cocktail, was an open, expensive, jeweller's ring box, with a tag attached saying, "Will you marry me?" and sitting in Aunt Alice's hand was a stunning, large, diamond solitaire. In taters around her were the remains of a pink cracker.

Shock, confusion and delight engulfed the room.

Irene looked at Jarrod, Jarrod looked at Vicky, Vicky looked at Aunt Alice, and Bill turned red as he gulped the air like a fish out of water.

Alice cried out in excitement, 'What a wonderful way to ask me! At Christmas, in front of my dear family. Of course my darling Stephano – it's a yes!'

For a man that was well and truly kippered, Stephano took it fairly well. What could he do? He smiled at Alice and his new family. Then he kissed and hugged Alice. And he played it cool.

Vicky was happy for her Aunt Alice, but deep down inside she secretly wished it was her, she tried not to make eye contact with Jarrod as she didn't want him to see the disappointment in her eyes. Still, Vicky was gracious enough to be the first to rush to her aunt and Stephano, wish them congratulations, and tell them how happy she was for them.

Irene scanned the table furiously. There were three pink crackers in total on the table, when there should have been one. How on earth had that happened? She knew it, she knew it! She knew it would go wrong. Damn.

Bill was completely defeated. What should have been a triumph of a plan was in tatters. It had been perfect. How could it have gone so wrong?

And poor Jarrod? He sat there, motionless, the expensive ring receipt burning a hole in his pocket, as the words stuck in his throat . . . "Will you marry me?"

* * *

Vicky was rather grateful to get into the car to go home. The car was cool whereas the house had been hot. It had been a rather odd sort of Christmas. She was pleased for her aunt, but the engagement had overshadowed the lunch a little bit. Jarrod had had stomach cramps all lunch and spent the rest of the day looking like he was coming down with something. Her mum had been cross at her dad. Even her nieces got it in the neck after Vicky had mentioned the crackers. She really didn't see what the fuss was about. They were just crackers. Her brothers had given up and gone back downstairs to play pool, and her sisters-in-law tidied and organised the way Vicky should have done to help her mum.

The nicest part of the day was that while everyone was busily involved with everyone else, Charles and Jenny were thrown together. They discovered their mutual love of Tchaikovsky over the turkey, and Puccini over Christmas pudding. It was really, rather lovely, but everyone had been too busy to notice.

It wasn't until Jarrod and Vicky were safely home that night that he really started to come back to himself.

'Darling.' Jarrod said, when they were cuddled up together on the sofa.

'Yes?' Vicky replied, safely snug in his arms.

'I was thinking, I want to do something special to celebrate our first kiss at New Year. I know we don't normally make a fuss, but I don't really want to go out. I'd like to stay in and cook dinner. Just us. Does that sound ok?'

'Oh, that sounds lovely. I'd love it. How thoughtful love.'

Jarrod smiled contentedly. He was many things, but he wasn't completely stupid. He'd paid a lot of money for Vicky's engagement ring, and while he deferred to his father-in-law's plan for the proposal, he certainly didn't trust Vicky's ring to a Christmas cracker, so he'd had the jeweller make up a zircon imitation. Just in case. The only problem would be if Vicky's aunt got the ring valued. It was unlikely he reasoned, and he had a feeling Stephano would smooth it over. Perhaps they'd never get the ring valued? Perhaps they'd move to Greece?

* * *

As it turned out Jarrod was right. Alice and Stephano moved to Greece, and had a lovely autumn wedding, with Jarrod's zircon engagement ring firmly on Aunt Alice's finger. It seemed Stephano was genuinely in love with Alice. Meanwhile Jenny and Charles decided life was too short to waste any more of it, and over a mutual love of Mahler, they were engaged in the summer and eloped the very next Christmas; like two young teenagers. And Jarrod and Vicky?

A week after his first attempted proposal, Jarrod cooked Vicky all her favourite things to celebrate their first New Year's Eve kiss. Then, during dessert, he got down on one knee, told her that she was his everything, and he couldn't imagine a minute in this world without her, and . . . would she be his wife?

Of course, Vicky said "Yes!" They embraced tenderly, kissed with love and happily called their respective families with the wonderful news.

3. TO MY BEAUTIFUL WIFE – AT CHRISTMAS X

Stuart passed round the champagne, except to his wife Fiona and their two children, Laurie and Sophie (a boy and a girl, aged seven- and six-years-old respectively) to whom he gave apple juice in pretty champagne flutes.

The Christmas tree sparkled in the ultra-modern living room of their large, newly renovated bungalow. The woodburner, which hung from the ceiling, distributed a cosy, cheerful, heat to the room. Wide glass doors looked out onto the immaculate garden, filled with unusual grass varieties; and bare, structural trees, which were shivering and waving their hands in the cold winter winds.

Stuart watched Fiona make small talk with his parents. He also noted the careful glance Fiona's parents gave her glass of apple juice. Fiona had been sober three years now. He was extraordinarily pleased with how far she had come since her post-natal depression with their second child. Not that the children were aware, their memories soon fade when they are that small.

A flashback came into Stuart's mind: He was pulling Fiona out of the bushes on their patio. She'd put a wine bottle through one of the glass doors. She had then passed out in the bushes. He could still smell the stench of vomit. He shuddered with the thought, and caught a look of his aghast face, frozen in memory, in the large ornate mirror over a side table. His face had a few more lines than his vanity would have wanted at his age, his black hair had a few flecks of grey, his eyes had a tinge of sadness at the edges, "But," he consoled himself, picking himself up by the bootlaces, "my beautiful Fiona has done it." As hard as it had been, she'd done it for him, for the family and most importantly for herself. Stuart was so proud of his beautiful wife.

Fiona's slick, black hair was tucked in an edgy, modern cut behind her ears. She wore an asymmetric, blue, merino jumper. Her pretty diamond stud earrings, a wedding gift from him, twinkled in the light of the Christmas tree. She was sparkling in the company of her family. She really had done so well.

Fiona took another sip of her juice, and from her seat on a cushion by the tree said, 'Let's open the presents!'

It had been an almost impossible job to keep the kids from demolishing the Christmas tree presents before lunch. Luckily the children had managed to just about occupy themselves with the presents from Santa. Just!

The immaculate living room started to drown under mountains of Christmas wrapping paper, as adults and kids alike tore off the paper in excitement.

Fiona picked up a particularly large present and exclaimed in delight, 'Oh! It's for me.'

'Read the label. Read the label.' Stuart said excitedly.

Fiona read: "To my beautiful wife – at Christmas x. I have always believed that you are one in a million and exceptional in so many ways. I see talent in you that you don't see in yourself. Yours, always, your Stuart xxx."

'Awwww . . .' came the collective response from everyone in the living room.

'Open it Mummy! Open it!' cried Sophie. She looked as if, if Fiona didn't start unwrapping soon, she would do it for her.

Fiona took a sip of apple juice, and carefully placing her glass on the side table behind her, ran her manicured fingers under the folds of wrapping paper at the edge of her present. The contents inside unfolded out in front of her.

'Oh!' Fiona said in surprise.

Stuart looked on in delight. His parents craned forward to try and make out what it was. Fiona's mum called out, 'Oh how thoughtful! How did you know about that?'

In front of Fiona sat two, black, fabric pouches, one of pallet knives the other of assorted paintbrushes. Also, within the package, were some packs of different coloured acrylic paints, a couple of small canvases and a large pink envelope.

Fiona carefully touched the pouch of pallet knives. She opened it and ran her finger over the steel blades as if she was saying an unsure, careful "Hello." to an old familiar friend. Her hand wandered to the pink envelope, which she opened with trepidation. Inside was a voucher for the local art shop.

Stuart said, 'I wasn't sure exactly what you would need, so I've got a voucher for the local art shop. They're also happy to exchange any of the other presents, just in case I got it wrong.'

Fiona was very quiet. She touched the pallet knives again and said in a quiet voice, 'No, no, they are just right.'

Everyone went very quiet. It seemed she didn't like the present at all.

Stuart leant over and rubbed her shoulder, 'I'm so sorry, I thought you'd like it. We can change it for something else if you'd like? Some jewellery perhaps?'

Fiona mum's face fell as she said, 'Oh, but Fiona, you used to paint so well. Surely you want to give it another go? You were so good!'

Fiona continued to stare at the pallet knives, something so familiar and yet so foreign, she was both attracted and scared of them at the same time. It had been so long. Fiona made her best effort to keep the happy Christmas atmosphere going. She smiled up at Stuart and said, 'Oh, it is such a thoughtful, wonderful gift. Thank you so much!' She reached up to kiss him on the cheek and everyone was delighted, as Fiona's mum talked at length about Fiona's wonderful artistic talents. It was such as surprise. Stuart's parents had no idea. It had been so long since she had painted.

Everyone said: "Wasn't it clever that Stuart had found out about that?"

* * *

Stuart watched his troubled wife eye the bundle of art materials as they tidied-up before bed. She was still starting at it as he turned off the kitchen light and took her hand to walk back through to the bedroom.

When they were alone in the still and quiet of the bedroom, getting changed in to their nightclothes, he ventured, 'Darling, I do hope it's ok. The present I mean. I didn't want to upset you. I won't be at all offended if you don't want it. I mean it if you'd like jewellery instead.'

Fiona stopped getting changed and came to him. She wrapped her arms round him and held herself there for a long moment. When she stepped back, she wiped away a tear and said, 'No, it's ok. It's just it's been so long. I don't know if I can do it. I don't know if I'm any good anymore.'

'Does it matter? As long as you're happy doing something you enjoy?'

'No. I suppose not.'

'Besides,' he said, kissing her forehead, 'you are perfect to me.'

He jumped into bed as Fiona went into the en suite bathroom to wash her face. Although he sounded confident, he really hoped he hadn't upset her. It's just that the abstract picture he'd found in the attic was quite frankly exceptional, and he wasn't even an expert.

* * *

They decided to put a heater in the large garden shed at the side of the garden, and turn it into an art studio for Fiona. She started to paint again, cautiously at first, but by the spring she'd gained enough confidence to purchase a few really large canvases. By May, Stuart was usually cooking dinner and getting the kids to drag her from the studio in the evening.

He watched with pride as her thin, bony, multi-coloured-paint covered hands demolished his lasagne. Fiona was glowing. She seemed so alive. Every day he couldn't imagine loving her any more than he did, and every new day he surprised himself with how much more in love with her he was.

Even the children had started to catch the painting bug and joined their mother in the shed on the weekends. Stuart could almost feel jealous at the lack of attention he was getting, if he had a smaller heart. As it was, he didn't notice at all and happily got on with the garden.

By the summer Fiona had painted nearly twenty beautiful pictures and their modern bungalow was filling with art.

Nervously Stuart suggested, 'Darling, have you ever thought of doing an exhibition?' Fiona froze in fear. He took her paint-splattered hands in his and started to gently persuade her. 'I'm no expert, and I know I'm completely biased, but your work is beautiful, it gives you so much joy, have you considered that it may also give others joy too?' Fiona faltered. She hadn't thought about it like *that,* spreading joy and happiness. Stuart could see he was onto a winner. 'You have so much love and kindness in your heart. Pass it on.' and with that he gently caressed the side of her face with his hands and kissed her forehead. 'It's your choice. I am always happy to have a house *full* of your artwork anyway.' he smiled at his joke.

Fiona cracked a smile too. She knew her husband too well. 'Ok. Who have you signed me up with?'

'Well . . .' said Stuart, fishing out his phone. 'There are three local galleries I've been in touch with. All of them sound great. I particularly like this one.' he flashed the website at her. 'They're called Waterside Contemporary Art and the gallery owner, Harvey, was particularly enthusiastic. He suggested a week-long "special" exhibition at the start of December. What do you think?'

Fiona let out a big sigh, as if she was letting go of a big, pent-up fear. She shook her head teasingly and pinched him, saying, 'I should have known better when you got involved!'

* * *

The autumn was frantic. Painting, photographing and varnishing. Apparently, every good artist had a website, so that had to get done. In the last few weeks coming up to the gallery launch, Stuart wondered when he might get his wife back, and if this really had been a good idea. Even the kids were starting to feel a bit neglected.

Stuart consoled them. 'This is really important for Mummy, and we need to support her right now.'

Sophie wandered out to the shed. Her mum was on the phone.

'Yes . . . Yes . . . Uh-huh . . . Yes . . . I can get that one to you tomorrow. I'll drop it off after the school run . . . Yes, that one has been fully photographed and is ready to put in the catalogue . . . Ok . . . Yes, speak tomorrow. Bye.'

'Who was that Mummy?' Sophie asked, taking some brushes out of a pot and flicking the ends.

'Don't do that dear.' said Fiona putting them back in the pot. 'That was Harvey.'

'Who's Harvey?'

'He's the gallery owner.'

'Oh.'

'Mummy, do you still love us?'

'Oh sweetheart. Of course I do! I'm so sorry I

haven't spent much time with you lately. Let me clean up now and come inside. What would you like to do?'

'Would you read some stories with me?'

Fiona placed her hand on her daughter's shoulder and smiling into her eyes said, 'I'd love to do that darling.'

Stuart returned from the shops to find Fiona and their children nestled on the sofa, the fire blazing and her sweet, soft voice reading Roald Dahl's *The BFG*. It was moments like this that made Stuart's heart melt.

* * *

Just as she'd promised, Fiona dropped off the painting the next morning.

Harvey, the gallery owner, was in his early forties. However, age seemed to have only bestowed him with more favours. He tended to wear his shirts a little too slim, but it showed off his athletic physique to the best advantage. His light-brown, wavy hair appeared to be nonchalantly loose over his forehead, in fact it took a careful regime of conditioner and non-gel-look gels. His scent was gently masculine, obvious but not offensive. His skin was tanned, hiding any wrinkles. Everything about Harvey was charming and attractive. And that wasn't by accident.

Fiona stepped out her car in her paint-stained jogging bottoms, and a scarf round her head to hold back her hair.

'Hey! How's our star painter this morning?' Harvey called out cheerfully.

Fiona shook her head good-naturedly as she replied, 'Ugh! Don't ask. So much to do.'

'Ah, nothing you can't handle, I'm sure. But hey, if you need any extra help, just give a call. I always have my mobile on me.' He took his phone out of his pocket and waved it just to prove the point.

They both walked around to the boot of the car to carry the painting inside. Once inside the gallery Harvey grabbed a Stanley knife and gently separated the tape to pull back the bubble wrap and reveal the painting inside.

He stood back and whistled appreciatively at the abstract painting, 'Wow! That's a stunner. I really don't think we're going to have any issue selling it. Fabulous.' he bear-hugged Fiona. 'The exhibition is going to be a fantastic success. I can just feel it.'

* * *

Fiona slipped the floor-length, teal-green, velvet dress over her head. Sitting on the edge of the bed she put on her royal-blue, strappy heels. She then glided over to the dressing table, put in her diamond studs and donned a pretty, silver bracelet; with rough-cut, aquamarine gemstones. Finally, she stood in front of the mirror to survey her efforts. Stuart hadn't taken his eyes off her for a moment. He sighed contently. He was so happy.

He was so in love.

'You look beautiful love.' he said.

Fiona turned to him, as if she only just realised that he'd been watching her. She flashed him a smile, 'Beauty is in the eye of the beholder.'

'Lucky me.'

She walked to him and flung her arms around him, as if she was shipwrecked and holding onto a rock in a storm. 'Thank you.' she said. 'I wouldn't be here without you.' She didn't mean the art exhibition that was opening tonight, and they both knew it.

Tenderly they kissed.

* * *

Laurie and Sophie had been given special dispensation to stay up late and attend the first part of the exhibition. However, as Fiona's parents would be there too, they only had a pass for the first-half and then they had to go home with their grandparents.

In the car to the exhibition, Laurie tried to persuade his parents to let them stay later. 'But I'm eight now. All of my friends at school get to stay up late.'

'No.' Fiona reiterated. 'And that's an end to it.' The kids gave up. They knew it was a battle they'd never win anyway. But it was worth a shot.

The gallery was lit up like a lighthouse beacon in the cold winter night. It was the first week of

December and Harvey had done a wonderful job of advertising the exhibition. The car park was already starting to fill up. Fiona felt nervous.

Stuart took his hand from the steering wheel, and squeezing her leg said, 'I have a good feeling in my bones about tonight.' It was the boost she needed. In the dark she smiled; and sparkling Fiona stepped out from the shell of worried Fiona.

Fiona was the star of the show. The abstract paintings were beautiful. Some were deep, sea-hues, with brooding blues and greens; others were bright, bold, sunset-colours in pinks and peaches. Everyone commented on her use of colour. It seemed strange to Fiona, because that's how she saw the world.

The exhibition was, obviously, a resounding success. Ten paintings sold on the night and there was interest in another five. Harvey said he'd never had such a successful exhibition.

As the guests started to leave, and the last few bottles of champagne had been opened, Fiona started to wind down. She felt tired. She was ready for her bed. This last week had been exceptionally hectic and she was quite happy to go home, put on her cosy slippers and dressing gown, and worry about techniques, orders and sales tomorrow.

Stuart sensed she was starting to flag and wandered over to her. 'You ok love?' he asked.

'Yes. Great. But I think it is time to go home.' she smiled wanly; she was flagging.

'Do you want me to get your coat?'

'No, I'll do it. I'll be back in a minute. Are you ok to double check the paperwork with Harvey?'

'Sure love. No problem.'

But Stuart couldn't find Harvey. Someone suggested he'd just gone outside for a smoke, but he couldn't find him outside either. Shrugging his shoulders, he decided it could probably wait until the morning.

Stuart scanned the room. He couldn't see Fiona either. Stuart wandered towards the cloakroom at the back of the gallery. He weaved his way through the cubist, white-walled labyrinth.

Stuart was about to enter the cloakroom when he heard, 'You are exceptional to me.' Stuart froze. In that moment his heart stopped. Peeking round the corner of the wall, his eyes confirmed what his heart had secretly feared these last couple of months.

There, as still as a statue, as beautiful as a Michelangelo, stood his Fiona. Light barely passed between her body and Harvey's, as he stood inhaling her breath. He raised his hand and pushed her hair back behind her ear as he bent down to place kisses down the side of her face.

Stuart's eyes burned, and a huge darkness opened below him as he felt as if he was falling from the world around him and all sense of reality.

Fiona's voice rang out clearly in the small, muffled room. 'If you ever touch me again, I will call the police and have you arrested for assault. Get. Off. Me.' She stood perfectly still. Her voice was as cold as winter ice.

Stuart's eyes were sore from staring without blinking, and his body was weak as he swayed slightly. An intake of air punched his lungs as he started breathing again. Just in time he stepped back as Fiona turned around – to an empty doorway.

'I'll destroy you.' Harvey said behind her. 'You'll never work in the art industry again.'

'Destroy me?' Fiona retorted with disgust as she turned to face him. 'You couldn't even come close.'

Stuart turned, and clutching at the white walls, managed to scrabble his way along the corridor. He lurched into the mens toilet, and just making the toilet bowl, was violently sick.

Back in the cloakroom, Fiona grabbed her coat and marched out, followed by the glare of a jilted Harvey.

Fiona entered the foyer and scanned the room for Stuart. A few of the last guests accosted her, wished her, "Happy Christmas." and again complimented her on her wonderful exhibition. Finally, Stuart appeared, looking a little white. He made his way over to Fiona, where they linked hands and gracefully begged their goodbyes.

On the car journey back both Fiona and Stuart were quiet. Fiona was still trying to push back her rage inside her chest. Stuart was trying to just focus on breathing and driving. He turned the air con on to "air-recycle" and hoped Fiona wouldn't smell the sick on his breath.

Finally, Fiona broke the silence. 'I know I'm an addict Stuart. I know I can become addicted to anything: sex, drugs, rock and roll.' she tried to make it a joke, but they both knew it wasn't. 'I know I'm susceptible *all the time*, but I also know that I wouldn't be alive without you and the kids. That's a fact.' She turned to him, as Stuart tried to hide the tears streaming down his face in the darkness. 'Can you accept that I may get addicted to my art?'

Stuart put on his best "normal" voice and squeezed her leg in the darkness as he said, 'Every facet of you is wonderful to me.'

* * *

It was time for the presents! The Christmas tree, decorated by Fiona, had large turquoise and gold baubles, and white twinkling lights. Tiny angels trumpeted from the branches as Laurie pulled out a card and passed it to his dad.

'This one's for you Dad.' he said.

'Thanks!' replied Stuart, reaching for it. The envelope was adorned with little painted hearts, each intricate and different.

'Oh! Read the card out loud!' Fiona interrupted, smiling.

Carefully Stuart opened the envelope, so as not to damage it. Inside was a little card with a watercolour picture of a boat. Obviously, it had been drawn and painted by Fiona. Inside the card was a cheque.

Stuart read aloud the message to the rapt audience around him: 'I'm sorry I've been a bit occupied this year. I blame you for giving me the paints. We all have a passion, so let me return the favour. These are the profits from my picture sales this year.' Stuart stopped reading aloud and looked at the cheque, his eyebrows rose in surprise as he did a double take. He continued reading, 'I thought we could use this money as a down payment towards a yacht; something you've always wanted, but we said we couldn't afford. I thought it could be something we could do together as a family next year. Yours, your Fiona x.'

Screeches erupted from the room, and Sophie and Laurie rushed to their dad.

'A yacht, we're going to get a yacht!' Sophie and Laurie shouted as they jumped up and down.

Fiona's in-laws were very impressed. Fiona's parents beamed with pride. Fiona smiled adoringly at her rock of a husband; her mainstay. Their eyes locked in the security of their love.

4. DRIVING HOME FOR CHRISTMAS

It was the last week before Christmas. The office had been getting quieter, the decorations were looking a little tired and the snow outside had been falling thick. Lilly and James had both worked at Leaper Enterprise for nearly five years. It was a large office of several hundred people, and although their offices were on the same floor, it was only at the coffee station that they talked.

James was quite tall and athletic, with dark-brown hair and clear-blue eyes. He was part of the environmental group, ensuring the company complied with government regulations. He was good natured, gentle and had a lovely, deep laugh.

Lilly worked a few offices down from him. She was a natural redhead. Although secretly she'd always fancied dyeing her hair pink, however, as that wasn't appropriate for her work as a personal assistant, she was never brave enough to try. Lilly had porcelain skin and striking hazel eyes. She was a little curvy as many women are. Lilly liked to dress in retro florals and A-line skirts. She was distinctive in her fashion sense.

Even though Lilly and James were quite different, they always seemed to stop to make coffee at similar times, and it was natural and easy for them to talk together.

As Lilly exited the ladies toilet, patting at her curly, red hair, James leaned back from the coffee machine to greet her. 'Your hair looks great by the way!' he called out teasingly.

Lilly gravitated towards him. She smiled politely but she wasn't her usual cheery self.

'You ok?' James said noticing.

She smiled wanly, 'Yeah.' Then she blurted out, 'I had to walk in this morning, in the snow. My car ABS system needs changing out. Not only is it going to be expensive, but they can't get the part in before Christmas. I was supposed to be travelling home Christmas Eve to see my family; to see my dad. I hate the thought of travelling on packed trains and taxis. I'm just not looking forward to it that's all.'

'Hey that sucks. What bad luck. Yeah, you need to get home to see your family for Christmas. Where are you heading?'

'Devon.'

'No way! My family are from Devon too! Although my parents live in Saltash now.'

They both stood in amazement at the similarity. How was it possible that after five years of chit-chat at the coffee point, lots of little silly jokes and pleasantries, that they really knew so little about each other?

'Look,' James continued, 'I don't want to intrude and all that, but I'm driving down myself Christmas Eve. Do you want to take a lift with me?'

And just like that it was decided that Lilly and James would drive down together.

* * *

It was a bit strange telling James, whom she'd known so long, her mobile phone number and home address, so that he could pick her up.

Lilly had quite a few presents and bags to load into James's estate car. Whereas James travelled light. Just a rugby holdall and no presents – apparently, he preferred to give gift vouchers. James didn't mind loading up Lilly's things. He was glad to be useful.

The snow was piled thick around them. Lilly was relieved James was driving. She wouldn't have wanted to drive in this weather.

They were off! As they headed down the motorway to the West Country, they spent the time singing and humming along to Christmas songs on the radio or chatting about this or that. Lilly was so grateful to be heading home. Her thoughts turned to her dad. She just wanted to wrap her arms around him, tuck in his blanket and make him a cup of tea. She was glad she didn't have the added stress of trains and taxis. It was really nice that James had offered to drive.

James, thankfully, was a steady driver. The snow

was very thick now. As they entered the West Country the motorway was down to one lane each way and the snow was drifting.

The radio interrupted their conversation: 'We have an amber weather warning from the Met. Office. Heavy snow is forecast tonight for all parts of Devon, Cornwall, Somerset and Dorset, with up to twenty centimetres of snow expected overnight in some areas. The temperatures are going to drop to around freezing tonight, however, with the cold easterlies we are forecasting this will feel more like minus ten-degrees centigrade. The advice is to wrap up and stay warm. The snow is predicted to continue falling until at least Boxing Day. Expect travel delays and road closures. The advice is not to travel.'

Lilly looked worriedly at James. 'That doesn't sound good. Do you think we'll be alright?'

James didn't want to worry her, but he also didn't like the sound of the forecast. He wanted to try and get her home to her family, he sensed that she particularly wanted to see her dad. He looked out into the last of the afternoon, as a peach-coloured, winter sun peeked through the snow clouds, and started to dip behind snow-covered hills.

'You're only just the other side of the moors.' he said. 'We'll be ok.' He wished it more than meant it.

* * *

They shouldn't have attempted to travel over the

moors. Lilly was heading for Tavistock. James's family lived in Saltash. The snow was falling thick and fast as they turned off just after Okehampton. The drivable road was little more than a lane between snow drifts. Not many people were crazy enough to be out in the bad weather tonight.

James turned the radio down, to minimise Lilly's distress over the weather warnings. Warnings weren't going to help him now.

They both sat in silence as the car slowly worked its way forward.

Finally, James spoke, 'Lilly, I'm sorry, I think we are going to have to stop somewhere tonight. I don't think we should continue. Is that ok?' Just as the words had left his mouth the car skidded on some ice under the tyres, and James struggled to keep on the small lane of road that was still useable.

Lilly clutched his arm with one hand and put her other hand over her mouth. 'That is absolutely fine.' she replied, worried.

'I think there is a pub up ahead if my memory serves me right. Let's pull in there. Ok?'

'Yes.'

It took them another fifteen minutes of careful driving, but eventually, through the heavy snow, they could see the cheery lights of The Fox and Hounds Hotel and Bar.

James carefully pulled off the road into the near empty car park.

'Are you ok?' he asked tenderly to a very cold and

very worried looking Lilly.

Lilly pulled the fur collar on her coat up a little higher and mustered her best smile. 'Feeling a lot better now.' she replied. 'Are you ok if I make a quick call? Just to let my parents know we're safe but we've stopped overnight.'

'Of course.' said James. He took his phone out and pretended to be checking his messages, so that Lilly wouldn't think he was eavesdropping.

'Dad? Dad? . . . It's Lilly . . . Lilly . . . I'm your daughter . . . Yes that's right, Lilly your daughter . . . Is Mum there? . . . Mum . . . Ok . . . Hi Mum! Look I'm really sorry but we have to stop overnight because of the snow, we should be there tomorrow hopefully . . . Yes . . . Yes that's right . . . How's Dad . . . Uh-huh . . . Uh-huh . . . Ok, well I've got to go, see you soon . . . I will. Love you too. Bye. Bye.'

* * *

The landlord and landlady at the Fox and Hounds had a policy of never turning a guest away, particularly in the worst snowstorm in ten years. They warmly welcomed the cold, tired travellers. They set up Lilly and James with adjoining rooms. There was steak and kidney pie advertised on the specials board for dinner – and nothing sounded more delicious to the weary travellers. There was a warm fire in the bar area, little nooks with built in benches, chairs and tables scattered about and a Christmas tree twinkling in the corner. Lilly didn't think she had ever seen such a welcoming hostelry.

Lilly and James decided to take half an hour to freshen up, then meet back downstairs in the bar area for dinner. By the time Lilly made it downstairs she found James already in one of the cosy nooks by the fire, with two glasses of sherry on the table and reading his Kindle. Christmas music tinkled in the background. Otherwise, the bar was completely empty.

'I hope it's ok.' James said motioning to the sherry. 'Just it seemed a little bit more Christmassy and I wanted to make the best of this.' He looked up hopefully at Lilly. "Gosh," he thought to himself "she really is very pretty."

Lilly had put on a little red lipstick to cheer up her attire. She had a fitted, dark-green, A-line skirt with a silk blouse and a cropped, tight-fitting, grey, cashmere cardigan. Her hair fell in large red curls round her face, she'd caught her hair at the sides with little pearl hair slides. She was the picture of femininity.

Lilly almost blushed and flashed James a kind smile, as James turned off his Kindle and stowed it away. To tell the truth she was bitterly disappointed not to make it home tonight. She wanted to see her dad. She feared that this was the visit when he'd finally forget her. But, because it was Christmas Eve, and she had a full suitcase of nice clothes, she decided to put on her lipstick, her nicest smile and try to make the best of things.

Besides James was easy company to be around.

The bar was empty except for the two of them. By way of explanation James continued, ‘The landlord has left the bottle of sherry on the bar for us to help ourselves. He said we are the only ones dining tonight, and dinner will be ready in ten to twenty minutes. He said he’d give a shout when it was ready. You don’t mind steak and kidney pie, do you?’

‘Not at all! I love it. To be honest anything warm and tasty is more than welcome tonight.’ she hesitated before she continued. She already knew the answer in her heart from looking out of her bedroom window before she came down, but she wanted dependable James to confirm the reality to her, ‘We’re not going to be able to get home for Christmas tomorrow, are we?’

James sensed her bitter disappointment, he would have done anything to protect her from the pain he was about to deliver, but to risk their lives was reckless. In all honesty he wasn’t going to be able to get out the car out of the car park, let alone drive it along the road. The car was already covered in a blanket of snow.

James touched her hand very lightly as he said, ‘I’m really sorry. The snow is really bad. I think we won’t be out of here before the twenty-seventh if I have to be honest. I’m really sorry Lilly, I know you wanted to see your dad. I wish I could have got you there tonight. I blame myself. I should never have tried to drive over the moors this evening. I’m lucky I didn't kill both of us to be honest.' and he shook his head at himself.

'Not at all James. You knew I wanted to get home. Hey, don't be hard on yourself. Look, I know it's a bit unusual but let's try and make the best of it between us? We can still have a nice Christmas, and this inn you found is great! It's so Christmassy!' Lilly smiled warmly at him.

James cheered a little knowing Lilly didn't completely hate him for messing up her Christmas. Just then the landlord called them through for dinner.

* * *

After their delicious dinner Lilly and James retired back to the warm bar. James grabbed the bottle of sherry off the bar and Lilly went to find a board game from the box in the corner. She came back with cards and scrabble. They settled on gin rummy. As James shuffled the cards Lilly looked out of the window onto the car park. James's car was surrounded by drifting snow and had a layer of snow over it. They were lucky to stop when they did. Lilly shivered at the thought of it, she tried not dwell on her disappointment. There was nothing she could do and she didn't want to spoil Christmas for James. It was an odd situation, but she just had to make the best of it.

The landlord briefly wandered over and enthralled them with reports of the snow drifts from the locals. He revelled in some scary and sensationalist stories of previous snowstorms, before finally leaving them to their evening. Lilly didn't want to risk being outside. What a Christmas!

James had seen Lilly shiver and put a few more logs on the fire. As she settled into the nook next to him, ready to play cards, he asked, 'Are you ok? Not too cold? Not upset about missing your family Christmas?'

'James you are a dear. I know you are concerned, and I know you wanted to get me home, but you made the right decision to stop here.' She smiled into his eyes as she said the nicest thing she could think of to make him feel better, 'Maybe it's fate, maybe I'm supposed to spend Christmas with you.'

Perhaps it was the sherry, or perhaps it was the extra log on the fire, but James felt all warm inside.

When they retired to their rooms that evening James was bold enough to give Lilly a peck on the cheek before bed. They both fell asleep warm, safe and happy.

* * *

Lilly picked out a particularly Christmassy dress the next morning. It was red with black-velvet swirls, fitted at the top and flaring out at the skirt, with an underlayer of black tulle. She wore some cute, black, Mary Jane shoes, with little cherries on the straps. She paired this with a little, black, cashmere cardigan and some little, cherry clips in her hair. Finishing with a flash of red lipstick she felt decidedly Christmassy.

She looked out of her bedroom window. She could she James's estate car covered in snow; almost up to the side mirrors where it had drifted. They looked like two ears poking out. It was almost funny. Lilly thought about the cold presents in the car, waiting to be opened. "No point in wishing for what you cannot change!" Lilly thought, trying to change her thinking and moving herself on. It was Christmas and it would still be lovely.

James was in his little nook by the fire. Reading his Kindle. He'd ordered coffee and croissants, and had them waiting for her. He was so thoughtful.

'What are you reading?' she asked.

'Oh, it's about Hillary's expedition to Antarctica.' James replied. Lilly wasn't surprised it was "sports" related. It was strange, they got on so well and had so much to talk about, but there were definitely some differences.

They enjoyed breakfast and cosied up in the nook to watch *Love Actually* on Lilly's iPad. At around eleven-thirty the first of the lunch guests made it through the snow to the bar. They hadn't come far, just from the houses on the opposite side of the road to the inn.

People stomped snow off their boots in the doorway, unwound scarves and shook their coats. They were a family of eight, obviously augmented by relatives staying for Christmas. Twenty minutes later two more families joined and an elderly gent, who'd bravely walked ten minutes through the snow to have a warm Christmas lunch and company.

It was quite nice to have other people around. Lilly took her iPad upstairs and came back down to join the jolly Christmas crowd. James was at the bar talking to a pretty blonde, who was wearing leggings, a fleece and a sports headband. They looked like a couple, Lilly thought with a twinge of jealousy. Lilly politely joined them and made small talk.

At lunch Lilly and James were sat at a table near the open fire in the dining room. James had his back to the room while Lilly had the luxury of looking out. She was still aware of the pretty blonde. Why did that bother her so? Lilly decided to be particularly charming over lunch. She was *almost* flirting with James.

James raised his glass of champagne over their Christmas puddings. 'I think we deserve a toast!'

'We do?' Lilly replied.

'Yes, to the most unexpected, surprising, and perfectly delightful Christmas I've had in a long time.'

Lilly raised her champagne glass to clink with James's glass and their eyes met with an easy warmth flickering between them, just like the little tealights that adorned the Christmas tables.

After lunch James suggested they venture out for a walk in the snow. Lilly didn't particularly fancy it, but at the back of her mind sat the sporty, pretty blonde who would probably jump at the chance, so Lilly had said, "Yes."

Wrapped up against the cold, James helped Lilly navigate her way through the snow drifts in the car park. They turned away from the main road and up a side road beside the inn. No cars had been along here today. Just a few footprints from winter explorers like themselves.

They walked up the lane until they found a gate overlooking the countryside. Stopping by the gate, James helped Lilly up, to stand on the slats and get a better view.

'Oh! It's stunning, isn't it?' said Lilly looking out over the white fields, snow-decorated trees and on into the distance and the snow-covered moors.

'Stunning!' James agreed next to her, as he surveyed the beautiful winter scene in front of them.

'I know you wanted to get me home, but really, I've had a lovely time this Christmas with you.' she said, as she turned her head to smile at him.

Without really realising it was happening, James leant his head gently towards hers and kissed her. His lips were so soft. He smelt of fresh, cool, male shower wash; like soap and cool mountain streams mixed together. He reached his hands up to her face and gently held her as he became more confident in kissing her. And she responded.

Kissing James was like warm, cosy fires and sparkling Christmas lights rolled into one. Lilly hadn't realised before that she'd wanted to kiss him so much, but now that it was happening, now that they'd started, she didn't want to stop . . . After a while, Lilly started to shiver with the cold.

'You're cold?' James said with concern.

'A little.'

'Let's go back. Here, let me help you.'

Lilly wiped her mouth with a tissue, then, laughing, delicately wiped off her lipstick from James's mouth too.

Arm in arm, Lilly and James re-entered the inn. Lilly confidently held James's hand as they headed to the bar for a post walk (post kiss) drink. Lilly noted with satisfaction that the pretty, sporty blonde turned her back on them. Lilly gave a little smile.

* * *

By the next morning the sun was in full force and the gritters were out. By lunchtime James had been out several times to survey the road and judged it passable.

'Are you sure?' Lilly asked worried. Part of her wanted to stay in this beautiful oasis with James, kissing. Part of her desperately wanted to see her dad.

James too looked a little sad to leave their happy retreat, but he wanted to get her back to her dad. 'Yes, the road is looking much better, we'll be fine.'

James took great care delivering Lilly back home.

They pulled up outside a ramshackle cottage. Snow and icicles were dripping off the thatch roof. James felt a little apprehensive to meet Lilly's parents. He hoped they'd like him. He grabbed some bags full of presents from the car, as he followed her into the house.

Lilly's mum greeted them at the door. She gave James a warm smile and offered him a cup of tea or coffee. Lilly briefly kissed her mum on the cheek as they wished each other, "Happy Christmas!" then she rushed into the house to see her dad, who was sitting in a chair by the fire, with a blanket over his knees. He was scribbling in a very small notebook and his glasses were partway down his nose.

'Dad!' Lilly rushed over to him, embracing him, then giving him a huge, squeezy hug.

'Oh! Hello!' he said, looking up in surprise. Looking blankly at Lilly he said, 'Who are you then?'

James watched Lilly's heart break into a thousand pieces.

'It's Lilly, Dad. Lilly. I'm your daughter.'

'Oh! Are you?' he smiled pleasantly at her, then turning to his wife he said, 'Sal, Sal, do I have a daughter?'

Lilly saw her mother roll her eyes at a question she'd heard hundreds of times before. 'Yes Dennis, you do.' she smiled wanly at them, then left for the kitchen to make tea.

James stood looking at Lilly. Tears streamed down her face. He came over and placed a hand on her shoulder.

Lilly's dad turned back to her. 'Oh. Well, hello. Nice to meet you.' He looked up to James and offered James his hand. 'Hello.'

James shook it and said, 'Hello sir, happy Christmas.'

Lilly's dad looked surprised. 'Is it Christmas?'

'Yes.' Lilly nodded sadly.

'Sal! Sal! Is it Christmas?' Lilly's dad called out.

A voice came back from the kitchen, 'Yes! I told you Lilly was coming for Christmas.'

Lilly's dad turned back to her, and said, 'Well thank you very much for coming. Please take a seat. I was just writing some notes on the granite used for the hearth of the fireplace here. It came locally from Haytor Quarry. It's a blue granite you know. I went to Haytor Quarry as a kid with my best friend Theodore from school . . .'

Lilly held his hand as she knelt beside him and listened to him. He recited with perfect clarity events from nearly sixty years ago. Next to her, perched on a little stool, sat James with his hand on her shoulder. Lilly smiled up at James through the tears, she was so grateful that he'd managed to get her back home to her dad for Christmas. Even though this was the year he finally forgot her.

5. MY CHRISTMAS ANGEL

Little Rowan played with his train set as his proud mother looked on.

'I love you, my darling.' she said.

''Es.' he said looking up at her, nodding and smiling.

Never had Maddie believed she could love a little person so much. She would do anything for this tiny, little human. She hugged him and bathed him. She chatted with him. They were so happy in their little unit of two. Their love was pure and their connection unbreakable.

There was only one thing that troubled Maddie. Her ex-boyfriend and Rowan's father, Darren. He was controlling and he was trouble. He had abandoned her pregnant. Maddie had been scared to do it alone, but with the help of her family she had successfully navigated being a single parent. For the sake of little Rowan, she had encouraged a relationship with his father (Darren had reappeared a few days after she had given birth). But she worried because every time Darren visited Rowan, Darren would become more aggressive and controlling towards her.

Maddie had reported it to the police: That she had found Darren in her bedroom, going through her personal belongings. That she had come home to find the cooker gas on, on two occasions. That she had caught him at the front door with a stolen set of house keys, and that she had to pay to have the locks changed again, with money she didn't have.

Maddie was frightened. Yet in her heart she loved Rowan so much she didn't want to separate him from his father. Secretly she hoped that Darren would eventually come to love Rowan as much as she did. Even though Darren didn't offer financial support, he did regularly visit Rowan, and she was glad for Rowan's sake. Darren seemed so attentive towards Rowan; he tried to play with Rowan's little trains and sing him lullabies. The only horrible part of it was, as soon as her back was turned, he was upstairs rifling through her things again and little Rowan was all alone.

Maddie was feeling more and more uneasy about the whole situation. It was just five days to Christmas. Maddie hoped that Darren had bought Rowan some presents this year. Although she understood that Rowan was still young enough not to notice.

The doorbell rang. It was starting to get dark. She had an unsettled feeling in her stomach.

Maddie looked out of the window. It was Darren. He was swaying slightly as if he was drunk. He motioned at her through the window to come to the door. Maddie looked at Rowan happily playing with his trains on the rug. It was nearly bath time. She wished Darren would go away. But surely it would be ok? He wouldn't hurt them.

Maddie opened the door to a cloud of alcohol fumes. Darren aggressively pushed the door fully open. Maddie jumped back in surprise.

Darren spat at her more than spoke to her as he said, 'Who is he? Who have you been with? They told me at the pub. I know all about it. Don't think you'll get any money off me now!' He was shouting. Maddie felt embarrassed that the neighbours would hear. He continued, 'I'm going to take Rowan away, and there is nothing you can do about it.' He motioned to little Rowan who stood motionless in the doorway to the living room. He was clutching a little train and looking scared.

''Ummi.' Rowan called with his arms outstretched. He started to cry.

'Who taught him to make that whining noise?' Darren spat at her. 'He's too soft. He needs to learn what life is really like.'

Maddie was scared. She thought quickly and said, 'Oh look!' she pointed behind Darren, 'The police!'

Darren span round wobbling and nearly tumbled over, as Maddie neatly slammed the door behind him.

They were safe for now, but it wasn't the end of it. He hammered and raged and stormed. Rowan ran to her crying. Like a little limpet he wrapped his tiny arms round her neck. He wasn't budging.

Shakily Maddie picked up the phone to call the police. This time at least, he had done something she could report.

* * *

Maddie hadn't been the only one to report him. The neighbours had too. The police interviewed her, and they discussed the situation with her. The difficulty was that as Darren had as equal responsibility for Rowan as she did, the police did not have the power to stop Darren seeing Rowan. Maddie was not going to allow Rowan to have unsupervised visits with Darren (secretly she was worried for Rowan's safety) and so the current visiting arrangement looked set to continue.

The female officer offered advice. She suggested mediation and gave Maddie a booklet with details of a child-contact centre. There was no way that Maddie could afford it. Maddie thanked the officer, sucked in a brave breath, and said that she was sure it was just a drunken incident and that she knew Darren loved Rowan. She thought it was just a blip, and it would all be ok when he was sober. The police officers exchanged looks and left shortly after.

That night, when it was quiet and dark, when Rowan was safely sleeping in his cot bed, Maddie allowed her emotions to surface. She had been holding it in. She had been so brave. But she was scared. First her body started to shake uncontrollably, then she curled into a ball, twisting into the duvet, then came the tears and the sobs. She buried her head in the pillow, so that she wouldn't wake Rowan.

From the far side of the bedroom, in the darkness, a sad set of eyes looked on. Their eyes welled up with tears, and tears dripped out of their nose. Trying to hold it together, they held themself tall, so that they wouldn't start sobbing. The partially open bedroom door pushed back a little more as two more sets of sad eyes joined them.

One thought to the other, "How is she?"

The first entity answered, "She suffers so much. She is a good mother. I wish I could ease her pain."

The third entity thought, "It is so hard to watch these lessons. But we cannot interfere. She has free choice. She must find a path through this."

The first entity replied, "Yes that is true my friend. But I am here to walk that path with her."

All three turned to watch the silently shaking, sobbing mass. Frightened, scared, apparently alone in this world, protecting her baby. Three pairs of eyes welled with sympathy.

The first entity broke away from the others and silently approached the bed. Opening their arms, they engulfed the frightened woman in a warm embrace.

Maddie's fear started to subside. She was reminded of her gran, who had passed nearly five years ago. She could smell her gran's subtle perfume and she could feel her warm embrace. She remembered that she was loved, even though she felt so scared and alone right now. Her soul slowly found peace in that memory and the tears started to subside.

The first entity turned to their friends with tears streaming down their face and their eyes met two similarly tear stained sets of eyes.

The second entity thought, “I’m going back to watch the child.” and quietly left. The third entity moved to stand quietly at the base of the bed. Like a sentry guard they watched Maddie sleep until the morning.

* * *

Maddie’s friend listened patiently before she replied, ‘I have to be honest Maddie. I think you are making a mountain out of a molehill.’ Maddie sat motionless and cold as her friend delivered her verdict. ‘Everyone at the pub knows how much Darren talks of little Rowan. He has photos of him on his phone that he shows everyone. He even put twenty quid in the children’s charity box at the bar because he said he wants to help kids. He’s a very generous guy. I have to be honest. I think the problem is you.’ She laid a reassuring hand on her friend’s arm. ‘Don’t get me wrong, I don’t think you know you are doing it. But subconsciously you are alienating Rowan from Darren, just because he left you pregnant. He didn’t have to stay, people break up all the time. Darren is doing his bit and is a doting father. I really don't think you can ask for more. I think you are being selfish quite frankly.'

Maddie sat cold. She couldn't speak. She just stared down at her untouched coffee. Her friend continued her judgement.

'Look. It's Christmas. Just give Darren some time alone with Rowan without you breathing over his shoulder. I've seen him around other children. He's a kind and thoughtful man. Just think about it ok? It's Christmas.'

Maddie's heart turned in on itself. The thought of Darren being left alone with Rowan chilled her.

From behind Maddie a hand gently reached out and rested on her shoulder, but neither Maddie nor her friend saw the gesture.

* * *

It was Christmas Eve. Maddie had had a wonderful day visiting family with Rowan. When they got home, she put out a stocking, milk and cookies for Santa. Not that Rowan really understood what was going on. More that she wanted to start the tradition.

Maddie stood over Rowan's cot bed, watching him sleeping peacefully. Behind her two entities watched quietly too. Maddie was a good mother. A third entity joined them and smiled at the loving scene before them.

The doorbell rang.

Maddie's heart sank. Part of her didn't want to

go, but it was only delaying the inevitable, and if she didn't go, he'd only make a fuss and wake up Rowan. Perhaps it was best to face this head on and get things out in the open.

Maddie stooped over the cot bed and gently stroked her sleeping son's cheek. Kissing her fingertip, she placed the kiss on the tip of his nose. Sighing deeply, she left the room.

The first entity turned to the third and thought, "Go now, you must go now, make sure they make the call. Be quick."

The third entity disappeared.

Maddie descended the stairs with a slow, heavy step. She had to brave. Who else would protect Rowan's interests? She looked at the hall clock. It was ten to eight. Opening the door ajar she saw Darren.

Apologetically he said, 'It's Christmas and I just want to sort things out for the good of Rowan.'

With a deep sigh she took the chain off the door and let him in. Maddie closed the door behind Darren and turned to show him through to the living room, only to find his hand round her throat.

'Idiot.' he said. 'Do you think I don't know what you've been saying about me? Trying to ruin my reputation. I gave you chances. I tried my best, but you just want to control me. Well, it's time I took Rowan. My turn.' he smiled.

Maddie gasped under his grasp. Her only thought was Rowan. She had to get her baby out alive.

He pressed her back against the wall and brought his face to hers. 'You going to try your tricks again? No police to save you this time.' His eyes were blank, black, emotionless, like a deep, bottomless well.

Maddie acted on the last thought her brain was able to provide oxygen for. She brought her knee firmly upward with as much force as she could muster.

Darren collapsed gasping to the ground.

Maddie scrabbled her way up the stairs as fast as she could. She had to get to Rowan. Just seconds behind her was Darren. Maddie burst into Rowan's room. She scooped him into her arms and backed towards the window. Darren came in and stood in the doorway, blocking their exit. His large frame was silhouetted in black against the hall light behind him.

Rowan was screaming in his mother's arms. She held him tight to her. All she could think was, "Someone please help me, he is going to kill us, please help, save little Rowan."

Darren reached into his pocket and pulled out a gun. Aiming it at Rowan's head he said, 'I think it's about time you experienced the pain you have caused me, ruining my reputation, trying to do things your way. I'm in control. Me.'

Maddie turned away from Darren, putting herself between the gun and Rowan, cowering her body over her screaming son.

The gun fired.

Rowan continued to scream. Maddie held him tight. What had happened? She turned around to see Darren holding the gun and looking puzzled. To his left was a large hole in Rowan's bedroom wall. He looked directly at her, took aim at her head, and fired again.

In the half-light the entity raised their hand. This time the bullet ricocheted to the right.

From downstairs Maddie could hear her front door being smashed in. She cowered by the window, her body over her son, she was speechless. Darren looked at the gun, looked over his shoulder and rushed into Maddie's bedroom. She could hear him trying to open her bedroom window.

Specialist police ran up the stairs. Two ran to her bedroom. One came directly to her.

Despite the insanity of the moment Maddie suddenly felt calm. As she held her screaming son, two sets of loving arms embraced them both.

* * *

It was the early hours of Christmas morning before Maddie finally fell asleep, on the blow-up mattress, on the living room floor of her parent's house.

Maddie awoke before everyone else, curled like a cat around the small body of her sleeping son. The events of the night before flooded back to her. Her face was wet with tears, and she was trying her best not to shake and wake Rowan. Her mind raced as she relived the memories. She whispered to herself, 'We're safe now. We're safe. We're safe.'

Maddie couldn't believe they were still alive. They were so lucky. Thank goodness her neighbours had called the police. Despite the mix up about the times. The police insisted they had received the call at ten to eight, saying that a gun had been fired. Maddie insisted again and again that Darren had arrived at ten to eight. She was sure. What did it matter though? Thank God the police had come when they did.

Little Rowan stirred beside her. His first words were, 'Wake-up. Wake-up 'ummi.'

'I'm awake my darling.' she replied. Maddie kissed his little forehead.

''Ook 'ummi, 'ook.' Rowan pointed to the sofa opposite them.

Maddie peered in the half-light. The morning sun was filtering its way through the curtains. But all she saw was an empty sofa.

'What is it my darling?' she asked.

''Ook, 'eople, 'eople last night.' Rowan pointed again.

Maddie's eyebrows knitted together with a puzzled expression. 'People from last night? Darling there's no one there.'

''Ook 'ummi, 'ook.' and Rowan smiled happily at the empty sofa.

* * *

Maddie wasn't religious, but when her parents offered if she and Rowan wanted to come to church with them, for the Christmas morning service, Maddie was positive she did. Holding her little person's hand as she walked to church with her parents, she repeated the same phrase to herself: "Thank you for my gift of life with this little person. I love him the most in the world. I will not forget this act of love. I will not forget it."

Beside each of them walked an entity. The second entity thought to the first, "We're not supposed to interfere really, you know."

The first entity thought back, "I know, but it isn't only humans that have free will. We do too."

"That is true my friend, we do." replied the second entity.

The first entity smiled at the loving mother and child as they replied, "I think they have a lovely story still to tell, don't you?"

"Yes my friend, I do." and reaching down the entity affectionately ruffled the small child's hair, just as the morning breeze bustled past.

6. SUMMER SUN AND WINTER SNOW

Debbie looked out onto the cold blustery December day. Little puffed up birds were fighting on the bird table over the tastiest nuts. They were strutting and puffing, pecking and pinching. "There's enough for you all little friends" Debbie thought. She enjoyed watching the birds and buying birdseed and nuts for them. One of her little guilty pleasures.

She hugged her mug of hot chocolate closer to her as she gazed over the frozen lawn, which was starting to gently thaw in the cold winter sunshine. She pushed back her dark-brown hair from her face with her thin, delicate fingers. Her other guilty pleasure was remembering back to her holiday this summer. It almost seemed like a dream. Sometimes she had to pinch herself to know that it had been real. But it had happened to her.

* * *

'Mum, I really think it would be a good idea for you to take a holiday.'

'I don't want to.'

Debbie's daughter looked at her despairingly. She spoke plainly when she said, 'It has been three years since Dad passed away. You are not destined to be alone. You have a big heart and I know you love all of us, but you shouldn't just be dedicating your time to us. You need to prioritise yourself and your happiness.'

Megan was right. Debbie did dedicate herself to her children and grandchildren, and she loved it. Nothing gave her more pleasure. But it was also true that she was scared to be "out there" and vulnerable. The young girl who had once looked back happily at her from the mirror now had a lined face and wobbly bits. She looked different. She didn't want to put herself out there and be rejected. She didn't want to be lonelier than she was now.

'Mum.' Megan brought her back to reality. 'Nick and I have researched this.' Megan dropped the cruise brochures onto the countertop. 'I know it seems a bit daunting, but this is a cruise for singles – everyone will be the same as you.' Megan tried her last argument to persuade her mum. 'We have all agreed, it will be our joint Christmas present to you.'

Debbie looked down at the brochures. It showed pictures of people coupled up or in groups. They were happy and laughing over dinner and wine or walking along sunny beaches. It looked lovely. Debbie's fingers lightly touched the brochures. She felt old and scared. She didn't feel courageous, young and brave anymore. How she wished she could call back the young girl she used to be.

* * *

That night Debbie had a dream. She was wearing a beautiful, floral-patterned skirt with a top in a mismatched pattern of the same colours. She looked and felt pretty. She swirled around as she danced and the skirt fanned out around her. She felt happy and free.

Debbie woke up laughing. She felt different. She felt as if she had touched the hand of her younger self to find she was still there.

Debbie turned on the bedside lamp and took a sip of water. On the bedside table sat a cruise brochure, calling to her. Perhaps she could be brave? As Megan had said, how could she expect things to change when she kept everything the same?

Debbie decided she would go.

* * *

Debbie's bravery fluttered a little as Megan, Nick (Megan's husband) and the grandchildren dropped her at the ferry port.

It seemed busy and everyone appeared to have a purpose and somewhere to go. But Debbie felt unsure and worried of the unknown. She'd never been on a cruise before.

Megan could see her mum waver and kept her mum focused to details. 'You have your passport and tickets?' Megan asked as she rested a kind hand on Debbie's arm and Nick got Debbie's suitcase from the boot.

'Yes.' Debbie responded, fishing the document wallet out of her handbag, and unzipping it to double check. 'It's all here.'

Megan spontaneously hugged her. 'I know you are going to have a fabulous time.'

Emotional sentimentality was pocketed aside as everything became business: check-in lounges; checking watches a hundred times; hugs and goodbyes, and finally boarding.

Everything seemed so well-organised and posh on the ship. Debbie was shown to her cabin. It wasn't large but it was fine for her. There were floor-length, sliding windows taking her out to a small balcony, overlooking the sea. She unzipped her suitcase. Her daughters had insisted on doing a makeover of her wardrobe. At first Debbie had been horrified, expecting crop tops and push-up bras. Instead, she had a suitcase of pretty, floral dresses and pastel-coloured cardigans. She chose to wear a particularly pretty, mint-green and pink, floral dress with a handkerchief hem. She pulled it gently from the pile to shake it out. She matched this with some dainty, mint-green, suede sandals and a cropped, mint-green, cashmere cardigan. She put in some small, gold hoops (the girls had insisted on this new addition to her jewellery collection) and grabbing her little shoulder bag, she left the cabin to go out on deck and wave goodbye to her old self.

* * *

The first night had been entertaining. Debbie sat at a table with twelve other people. All with different stories. They shared photographs and talked about children and grandchildren. The gentleman to her left had recently started to paint and certainly had a passion for it. Debbie didn't like his pictures though. They were a little too dramatic: with red and black paint slashed across the canvas. He seemed such a gentle, kind man. It was surprising really what lies inside some people, she mused.

The lady to her right was quite fashionable. She seemed so "with it" and knowledgeable of current fashions, trends and technology, that Debbie wondered why she was on this singles cruise. As they talked Debbie realised that beneath the lady's platinum-coloured hair was a scared, little girl, to whom no man would be good enough, or safe enough, or match her first husband. Debbie wondered if she too was a little like this? Did she not compare everyone to Derek? Was anyone, ever, going to be good enough?

Generally, Debbie found that she gravitated towards people who loved birds, just as Derek had. She was endeared to people who were good at carpentry, just like Derek. But as she looked around the table of new faces, Debbie saw lots of new, different people, each lovely and unique in their own way. Debbie realised there would never be another Derek, and she had the choice of staying alone, or being brave and discovering what was unique about someone new.

* * *

Debbie had a lot to think about as she retired to her cabin that evening. She had left her artist dinner companion enthralling a group of ladies with his latest works. Which, judging by the pictures on his phone, looked quite daring and a little too exposing. Not quite her cup of tea. However, the evening had been fun; she had laughed and thoroughly enjoyed herself.

Debbie undid the buckles on her strappy, silver-coloured shoes. They only had a little kitten heel, but her feet were puffy and tired. She was ready for bed. As she drifted off to sleep, she let her mind wander. A thought popped into her head and asked, "What would your ideal man look like?"

* * *

Debbie awoke excited for the day. They were due to stop at a Spanish port that afternoon; the first stop. After breakfast she decided to take a breath of fresh air on deck before her scheduled dancing class.

Debbie looked out over the dark-blue mass of water swirling around the boat. She inhaled the salty air and fresh wind. She swept her dark-brown hair back from her forehead and let the sun fall on her face. She felt at peace.

'I see I am not the only one who enjoys the sunshine.' a foreign voice said beside her. His accented voice sounded like words rolled into dark chocolate and toffee. Debbie opened her eyes to see a tanned, handsome gentleman standing not far from her. He had wavy, brown hair and dark, chocolate-brown eyes. His sunglasses hung from his light-blue, linen shirt and as he smiled to greet her, she noticed his huge, soft, brown, paws of hands were encircled by a chunky, silver watch.

'My name is Eduardo.' he said as he smiled at her.

She smiled back to him and shook his proffered hand. 'It is lovely to meet you. I'm Debbie.' she said. And for the first time, in a very long time, she didn't feel tired and wrinkled, instead she felt young and free.

It was quite a pleasant surprise to find Eduardo had also signed up for the dancing that morning. They didn't dance together much as the class instructor kept the partners rotating. However, she found herself looking forward to when she danced with Eduardo. His hands were so soft and warm; it was like dancing in the sunshine on a warm summer's day.

It turned out that Eduardo was also going on the same port excursion as her. Naturally they fell in step together as they walked around the markets. She couldn't help but be impressed when he conversed in his native tongue. Eduardo haggled and tried to get the best prices for the gifts she selected to take home to her family. They laughed and talked. The time slipped away. It all felt so easy.

And as easily as that, Debbie and Eduardo were together. They did everything together; arranging to meet before dinner, meeting at the same time for breakfast, taking a walk together after breakfast along the decks. Like naughty school children they missed prebooked activities if they weren't attending the same classes. Preferring instead to spend the time together.

Debbie and Eduardo also attended the same excursions at the ports, rearranging if necessary. Each excursion was like a little adventure just for them. When they climbed the Greek monuments, Eduardo held Debbie's hand, to safely guide her along the rocky paths. When her hand connected with his, it was like a warm, soothing hug in a touch. Debbie felt so at ease with him. Eduardo bought her ice cream when the sun was too hot. There was no awkwardness or wondering, "Will he call back?" They looked happy together in their own sunny, little world.

* * *

Debbie had fallen so easily into Eduardo that she didn't think about time, and she didn't think about *after.* However, all too soon it was the last night and the last dinner. Reality started to creep up on Debbie as she selected her outfit.

Debbie had kept the best dress for last. When she had first tried it on at the department store, she thought it had been too much, but when she left the dressing room her granddaughter's face said it all.

'Oh Granny.' the little girl said in amazement. Her eyes were wide open, unblinking, dazzled by her grandmother. 'You look like a fairy princess.'

Seeing herself through her granddaughter's eyes was like a magical spell being cast on her. In this dress she felt like a princess, although it was very much a woman's dress.

The dress was heavy-weight and fell from her shoulders to the floor. It was covered in silver sequins. The back was cut low, very low and had a cowl at the base. The top of the back was pulled together by a thin sequin band. In contrast the front was cut modestly high. The princess line skimmed her body and made the most of her small breasts. She had been instructed by Megan to pair this with her new, zircon, droplet earrings and nothing else. Debbie styled her hair loose with a slight wave. Large, dark-brown curls fell over her shoulders and hid the sequin band over the back of her dress. Debbie looked stunning.

Debbie had arranged to meet Eduardo on the third deck, in the drinks lounge for some predinner drinks. As she carefully walked along the corridors, gently stepping in her strappy, silver sandals, she drew admiring glances. She was aware of the backward looks and stares. It made her feel attractive and uncomfortable at the same time. It had been a long time since she had drawn a backward glance from a man. She was also excited to know if she would draw the same attention from Eduardo.

A kind gentleman held the door open for Debbie, as she entered the drinks lounge. As he held the door he struggled for a witty opening line, but his moment was past. Debbie thanked him and glided towards the bar where Eduardo was seated. Right next to him sat the platinum-blonde from the first night. She had her hand on his arm and was leaning towards him provocatively.

Debbie's cheeks burned and her step faltered. She felt as if a bag of jelly beans had been upturned in her chest and her breath quickened. This was new. She hadn't felt *jealous* in a long time.

It was only when she was nearly upon them that Eduardo turned to look at her. It was like the sun coming out from behind a cloud. His dark, chocolate-brown eyes fully fixed on her as he drank her all in.

The platinum-blonde stopped talking mid-barrage, noticing that he wasn't noticing her anymore. She turned to Debbie, her mouth dropped, then her brows came together in a scowl and her lips curled as she finally spat out, 'Aren't you a little over-dressed for dinner?' The comment was as bitter as lemons, but neither Eduardo nor Debbie heard.

Eduardo got up from the bar stool and slowly came towards Debbie. He couldn't take his eyes off her. Gently taking both her hands in his, he lightly kissed her on the cheek.

'You look beautiful.' he said simply. And he was right. Debbie looked stunning.

The platinum-blonde made one more attempt to break their connection, 'Eduardo and I were just talking about . . .' But no one was listening.

* * *

Debbie came back to the moment. She looked out on the cold December morning. She watched the little robins bobbing on the bird table. Guiltily she closed the memory box in her heart. She tried not to think of it again today.

Debbie and Eduardo had made plans to meet after the cruise. They had talked on the phone and written letters. But it seemed that the cruise had been a momentary break for Eduardo from his busy life. Soon after, the sale on his house in the UK completed and he returned to Spain. As he had children and grandchildren in both countries, both locations had a pull on him.

They had planned to meet up before he left, but due to complications to do with the move he couldn't make it the two hundred miles to see her.

And that was that. Her beautiful moment of summer sun.

* * *

Megan, Susan (Debbie's other daughter), respective husbands and grandchildren waved Debbie goodbye as she drove away from the large, four-bedroom house. It was only a few minutes down the road to the quiet of Debbies house. Whereas Megan's house was full and they were busy waiting for Santa to come. The young cousins were peeling off the walls with excitement. Yes, she'd leave them to it tonight. She would be more than happy to play with what Santa brought tomorrow morning.

It was dark. The houses were lit with twinkling fairy lights, and pretty Christmas trees peaked out from warmly lit windows. As Debbie turned off the main road, snow started to spot on the windshield. It has been promising to snow all day; cold and crisp with a few menacing dark-grey clouds drawing together at dusk.

Debbie pulled into her cul-de-sac, which was full of cars from the extra Christmas house guests. She weaved her way through to her driveway and pulled up outside her home. The snow was falling heavily and it twinkled in the glare of the garage security light. She wandered up the path to her hous, which was prettily lit with hanging icicle lights. The lit Christmas tree in her living room called out invitingly from the front window, "Come in, come in!"

It wasn't until her key was in the lock and she was about to turn it, that Debbie realised the garage security light had flicked on behind her. She turned around sharply to see . . .

Eduardo. Wrapped in scarves and shivering slightly, but sill radiating his own brand of warm, Mediterranean sunshine.

'Debbie?' he ventured.

'Eduardo!' she was stunned. Was this some strange dream or a hallucination? She had been thinking of him too much lately. She was lonely. She blinked. No, he was still there. A solid person.

'Eduardo?' she said again.

He rushed to her. They needed no re-introduction. His soft lips met hers. They kissed deeply and passionately. There was no awkwardness. It was natural and beautiful. Their bodies intertwined as he pressed her back against the door and snow collected in their hair.

After a while, after his lips and his heart had said, "Hello." he pulled back a little. He reached up to her face and caressed her cheek. He looked at her tenderly in the twinkling of the icicle lights.

'I've been waiting for you for three hours in the car, in the cold. It was supposed to be a surprise, so

I didn't want to call. I have champagne and flowers in the car. Your neighbour assured me you would be back. I think they will think I'm a stalker!'

They both laughed. Debbie didn't care about the neighbours.

She looked at him intently. 'I've missed you.' she said. Her heart had ached for him for months now. She thought she'd never see him again. She wasn't angry. She had so wanted to bask in the warmth of his sun, she had longed for him and now, here he was.

Eduardo looked at his feet and said quietly, 'I know. I'm sorry. I spent every moment since we parted thinking of you.' He looked back at her. 'I was scared. After Lucinda left me for another man, I was heartbroken. I didn't think I would ever trust or ever find love again. I've had relationships before, but I couldn't stay. I was scared of getting hurt again. Then I met you. And I just didn't think my heart would survive being broken twice.' He brushed some snow back from her hair, 'I love you.'

'I love you too Eduardo.'

They kissed again. Tenderly this time. Secure in their unit of two. The snow fell lightly on their heads like little winter wishes finding their mark.

When their lips parted again Debbie said, 'Well I guess it is too late for you to travel anywhere. You can stay . . . in the spare room.'

Eduardo smiled. 'That would be my honour.' he said.

'Would you like to come to Christmas lunch

tomorrow and meet the family?'

'If I wouldn't be in the way, I'd love to.'

'Oh you won't be in the way. Besides, you might not know it, but you are my Christmas present from the family.'

He looked at her quizzically and she tiptoed to kiss his forehead. Opening the door, they tumbled inside like a pair of teenagers. Outside the winter night sighed contentedly, snow flurries danced and a little jingle of bells tinkled on the breeze.

7. THE OTHER SIDE OF THE (CHRISTMAS TRAIN) TRACKS

Three boys stood on the bridge over the railway line, waiting for the Christmas Special steam train to pass by underneath. There was supposed to be a Santa on board. Not that they'd ever been. Or that they believed in Santa anymore. They were too grown up for that.

The boys were aged seven, nine and twelve. You could tell they were brothers, not just because they looked a little similar: the same auburn hair, pale skin and hazel eyes as their mum. But because they had the same, short, "home hairdresser" haircuts; the same polyester, padded, winter jackets – just in three different sizes; and the same mannerisms.

The road crossing the bridge over the railway was only lightly used by traffic, but that didn't stop the boys punching each other in play fights across the road, and scuffling with each other as they waited for the train to pass by underneath.

John, the youngest, loved trains. He'd begged his eldest brother Michael to bring him. Paul, his middle brother, was fairly easy-going and didn't mind. Michael felt some responsibility as the eldest to accommodate John's wishes, so they'd all gone.

Sometimes, when John was upset or feeling out of sorts, his mum would console him with: "One day we'll take a trip on the steam train – eh?" But they never did. There was never enough spare money. It was ok, as he understood that the essentials like the electricity bill and food came before luxuries like riding on steam trains – but still. He didn't tell his elder brothers, but when they went to sleep at night, in their shared bedroom, he would often imagine as he lay there waiting for sleep, what it would be like to ride on the train . . .

John would stand on the platform with his mum and brothers. There would be an old man with a large tummy, looking a little like the Fat Controller (although he knew *Thomas the Tank Engine* was for babies, so not very like him). Another man in a blue suit and matching cap would usher them on board, and they would sit around a table by a window. As it was just the four of them, they'd all fit; just as if it was made for them. Then the whistle would sound, the engine would puff, the wheels would creak and the carriages would jerk, as the train slowly started to move out of the station, and smoke issued from the train's funnel. "Chuff, chuff." Gathering speed the wheels would turn. "Chuff, chuff, chuff." From the engine the fire would burn. "Chuff, chuff, chuff, chuff." Faster and faster along the track, "Whoo, whoo!"

John came back to now. His brothers had been collecting pinecones to throw at the train when it passed. There was no point telling them not to as they wouldn't listen to him, so he grabbed a few to join in. Only he knew he would probably miss because he didn't really want to throw pinecones at the train.

'Here it comes!' shouted Paul in excitement.

The boys jumped up and down as they waited for the train to pass by. Michael went to the edge of the bridge and a little way down the side of the embankment. Paul went with him. John stayed at the top of the embankment. Although he wanted to get closer to the train, he didn't really want to attack it.

John watched in awe as the train puffed towards them. Steam and smoke gushing out. The distinctive "Chuff, chuff, chuff, chuff." The sound of the wheels turning; bending to the will of the powerful engine. He waited for the smell. He knew it by heart. He stood transfixed. The train blew its whistle at the boys, and his brothers jumped up and down with glee, taking their best aim as the carriages passed by . . . "*Smack, smack, smack.*" went the cones as they bounced off the windows.

* * *

'What was that Daddy?' said Ella, as she jumped in

her seat. Another pinecone hit the window.

Her father put a protective arm around her and peered out of the window over the top of his glasses. 'Just some naughty kids.' he said tutting. 'Someone should be watching them. They shouldn't be left to roam making trouble.' He had a good mind to report the children to the police. However, his thoughts were interrupted.

'Ho! Ho! Ho!' said Santa as he stepped into the first-class carriage.

* * *

Not long after a car came whizzing round the corner and over the bridge, scattering the boys. John dropped his unused pinecones. They collectively decided they'd better head home before their mum told them off for getting killed.

Entering the housing estate, they walked the pavement as a posse, back to home, back to mum. Old Mrs Horrel stopped the boys as they passed her front garden.

'Michael!' she called. 'Michael!'

Michael turned around and came to the gate. 'Hello Mrs Horrel.'

'Michael, be a good boy and pass this to your mum, would you? I said I don't use it anymore, and she said she was thinking of doing something with her hair for Christmas.'

Michael gratefully received the pack of hair dye. 'Thanks Mrs Horrel. That's really nice of you. I'll give it to Mum.'

'Good boy.' she said as she winked at Michael and Paul, before ruffling John's hair and clopping back down the path with her stick.

John wished he'd had a wink instead of having his hair ruffled. He styled it carefully with water every morning, just like his brothers, and he hated it when people messed it up.

The boys walked down a side alley to the back of their mum's semi-detached house. Or rather, not their mum's house, the council's house. It didn't really matter, it was where mum was and that meant home.

Pulling their boots off on the back doorstep, they bashed their boots on the concrete to get rid of the worst of the mud before coming inside. Michael made them do it. He said Mum worked hard enough. John surveyed the back garden with discarded footballs and rusting bikes hidden in the uncut grass from summer. It didn't really make sense to him. But Michael said he had to do it, so he did.

Jenny was in the kitchen drinking coffee and reading a dog-eared magazine.

'Oh good,' she said, 'you're home. I'll start tea.'

'What have we got?' asked Paul.

'Pasta-cheese ok?' their mum replied.

All the boys made "Yumm." sounds. They loved pasta-cheese. Even though they had it a lot, it was always welcome.

'Mrs Horrel passed me this for you Mum.' said

Michael, handing her the packet of hair dye.

On the front of the packet were the words "Perfect Peach" in big curly letters. 'Oh fabulous!' their mum said, looking pleased, 'I've been wanting to do something to spruce up my appearance. I've really fancied pastel colours for a while. That's really nice of her.'

John watched his mum go to the hall mirror and puff and preen her hair. He was glad she was happy. She'd look really nice with some colours on her hair.

'Have you had a good time out playing?' she shouted back through to the kitchen.

'Yes!' Michael replied, as he reached into a cupboard to get out a huge bottle of what proclaimed to be orange squash. Paul reached into a different cupboard for three beakers. John sat at the table fiddling with the packet of dye, testing to see if the box might just open by accident, so that he could see what was inside.

Michael passed a beaker of squash to him and took the packet of dye off him, placing it on the side of the worktop.

Their mum came back into the kitchen to boil the pasta. As she passed each boy, she gave them a little kiss on their heads.

'Good boys.' she said. 'Mummy loves you.'

* * *

That night John dreamt of trains. He was on the

"Santa Express" steam train. It was a little like the *Polar Express* but they'd lost the DVD, so he had to improvise in his dream to sort of recreate the story. It was somewhere between the local volunteer steam train and a massive locomotive heading to the North Pole.

There were other children, just like him, playing on the train. Santa came into their carriage.

'Ho! Ho! Ho!' he said, as he entered through the carriage door, several rows in front of John.

His was a big, old man, with a round tummy and a red suit with white fur. In many ways he looked like the Fat Controller (not that John watched *Thomas* anymore) but John couldn't quite be sure if he had a bald head or not, due to the big red hat that covered it.

'Ho! Ho! Ho!' said Santa.

John watched as Santa approached the first child three rows down. It was a little girl, about the same age as John.

Santa knelt before her and said, 'Ah! Little Alice. What would you like for Christmas?'

The girl replied like a rapid-fire shotgun with a list of toys John could only dream of: 'I want a Movie Magic Studio with the dolls; I want a tablet – but a big one, so I can store more games; I want a Polly Pocket Rainbow Funland; I want some princess dresses for my dressing-up box; I want a tent for my bedroom to play in; a new Barbie and Barbie van; a barking dog toy – you know, like the one my friend Trish has; and some sweets and chocolates as well. Thank you Santa.'

'Well,' said Santa, chuckling a little, 'that's a big list. You must have been a very good girl this year!'

'Yes.' she replied confidently. Santa patted her on the head and moved a row forward.

Big list! Thought John. That sounded like a whole toy shop. It sounded like more toys than he and his brothers had altogether. As he watched Santa talk to the little boy two rows in front of him, it dawned on John (in his dream) that Santa might ask him what he'd like. He felt a bit strange at the thought. He'd always written letters to Santa. They all did at the start of December, but he knew that you didn't get all the things on your list, you only got a few. Santa was probably just being nice to the girl with the big list. He shook his head with experience. She'd be lucky to get a Polly Pocket.

Suddenly Santa was before him. He knelt down in front of him. Smiling. John hadn't had time to think yet.

'Ah, young John.' said Santa.

John reasoned that obviously Santa knew his name as Santa knew everything. Even if he'd been good or not. 'Merry Christmas sir.' said John.

Santa smiled, 'And what would you like this Christmas?'

John hadn't really had time to think, so he just blurted out the words as they formed in his head. 'I really like trains Santa, I like steam trains. I'd like to ride on a steam train or have a train set that has batteries, so it goes round on the track.

But,' he paused wisely, 'I don't think Mum has much money this year, so I think it is better to ask for a turkey, because then we can all share it.' He clarified; 'I mean me and my brothers and my mum. We all love having roast and it's really nice when we eat as a family.' He nodded his head as the decision was made. 'Yes, could I have a turkey for our Christmas lunch please Santa.'

Santa knelt very still in front of the little boy. 'Of course you can have turkey for your Christmas lunch my young friend.' Santa placed his hand on John's head, but much to John's delight he didn't ruffle his hair. In a soft voice he said, 'You are a rather exceptional young man. You have a special place in the world. I hope you know that you are very lucky to have your mum and brothers who love you.'

John replied confidently, 'I know Santa. We love each other very much.' Proudly he said, 'We're a family.'

Santa nodded wisely, 'Indeed you are.'

* * *

John felt a bit odd the next morning, thinking about the dream while brushing his teeth for school. Why did he ask for a turkey instead of a trip on the steam train? He decided that's he'd write another letter to Santa during school today and post it on the way back home. He needed to clarify that it was a steam train trip that he wanted.

As it happened it looked like turkey wasn't going to be available this Christmas anyway. The television in the living room shouted out the news headlines while the brothers sat eating their oats before school:

'Our top news story. No turkey for Christmas! A recent outbreak of bird flu at two farms in Kent, who are both major suppliers for supermarket Christmas turkeys, mean that turkey is set to be a rarity for Christmas lunch this year. We now go over to our reporter, live at the Mr Matthew's Farm, in Appledore.'

'Mum!' Michael shouted through to the kitchen.

'Yes love?' came the reply.

'No turkey this year! It's on the news.'

Jenny came through with her arms folded as she listened to the news article. She didn't know if she was relieved or disappointed. 'Oh well. Chicken it is then!' she said, as she tried to make light of it to the boys. 'Time to get to school now.'

The boys finished their oats and put the bowls in the kitchen sink. Michael headed straight out to meet his friends and walk to the big school. Jenny helped John and Paul with their school things, and exiting the house she carefully locked the door.

* * *

Paul confided to John as they waved goodbye to their mum at the school gate, 'I don't think we'd have had turkey anyway, so don't be too disappointed.'

'Is it because of the electric?' John asked wisely.

'Yeah, I think so, also Mum's boss is refusing to pay the overtime Mum did.' He looked cautiously at his younger brother. 'She might not be able to get us the presents we wanted this year,' Paul softened the blow, 'but I overheard her say to Michael that she knew Santa was definitely coming with his presents, because he always comes to the good kids and we are such good boys.'

John nodded in affirmation. At home he always wiped his feet and banged the mud off his boots, like Michael told him to. He brushed his own teeth and took his clothes down to the washing machine when they were dirty. He'd done his bit this year – not that he believed in Santa, of course.

* * *

That evening Jenny motioned Paul upstairs to her bedroom and closing the door she sat him down on her bed. Taking his hands, she said, 'Paul, you have always been very good to your brothers, but I need to ask you something and this is completely your decision to make. Your father has sent fifty pounds for your Christmas present this year. I am having difficulty getting my boss to pay for the extra overtime I did, to pay for your Christmas presents. Would it be ok with you if I spent this money on presents from Santa for all of you? I think John still believes in Santa. I'll try and get something from me to you all later in the year. What do you think?'

Paul, just like Michael, was an old head on young shoulders. He reassuringly patted his mum's hand and said, 'It's ok Mum. I think the best thing to do is buy stocking presents for us all with the money. John says he doesn't believe in Santa anymore, but I secretly think he does because he was talking to him in his sleep last night.'

A small tear escaped Jenny's eye at Paul's goodness and she had a lump in her throat. She was a lucky mum to three wonderful boys.

'I still have hope my boss will pay me. I have a few gifts on hold on Gumtree. Let's hope I don't have to do this. But I really appreciate your kindness if I do.' She kissed the back of hands and rubbed his shoulders as they left her bedroom saying, 'You're a good boy. You all are.'

* * *

Everyone at school was talking about the turkey shortage. That weekend John brought it up with Michael. They were back at the bridge over the railway tracks, waiting for the steam train.

'Michael. Do you think we'll have turkey this year?' John asked.

'Nah. I don't. Don't think many people are getting turkey this year.' Michael expertly threw a pinecone at the tracks to test his aim.

'Oh.' said John a little sadly. He knew the answer

really, it was just, after his dream with Santa he'd hoped . . .

Paul added, 'But Michael's got a plan, haven't you Michael?'

'Yeah.' Michael said. 'I've been doing a few errands for Mrs Horrel and I've saved some money. I've got enough for a frozen chicken and maybe some Christmas cake. I thought we'd surprise Mum on Christmas Eve, so that she doesn't have to worry this Christmas.'

John smiled. He could taste the roast chicken already. Delicious. Just then, in the distance, they heard a, 'Whoo, whoo!' The boys jumped up and down in excitement, waiting for the train to pass underneath.

* * *

John and Paul met in the playground to discuss Michael's plans for Christmas and what they could do for Christmas presents for their mum. They couldn't buy anything but they could do jobs round the house and they could make things.

Paul had been working on a jewellery box. He'd found an old wooden box at the tip and he was gluing on little white stones that he stolen from a drive in the posh part of town. Michael had his plan of the frozen chicken and the Christmas cake. John decided he would draw a picture. He was quite good at art. He would draw a train.

As they sat at the edge of the playground one of

the new girls came over. She'd joined in September and was in the class above John. She was from the posh part of town.

'My dad said he's going to report you to the police.'

'What! What for?' said Paul cockily, putting his arm protectively around his little brother and secretly wondering if it was for stealing white gravel stones. He didn't want to go to prison.

'Throwing stones at the steam train.'

'They weren't stones. Anyway, it wasn't us.'

'Was.' said Ella confidently. She looked them up and down. Then, pulling her pink, duck-down jacket a little tighter round her skinny body, and flicking her blonde hair, she left to go back to playing with her friends.

John was worried. 'Do you really think they'll report us to the police? They might take us away from Mum.' Somewhere in his mind there rose a fear that this had happened before, but he couldn't quite remember.

Paul squeezed him a little tighter. 'Don't worry about it. Mum and Michael dealt with that a long time ago. You're safe now.'

* * *

Jenny hadn't had the best of luck in love. Her husband, her first love, had died in a car accident when Michael was only one. His life insurance policies covered the house. Although Jenny was financially secure, she was lonely.

Next came her fiancé, the helicopter pilot. They were due to be married in the summer when Jenny fell pregnant in the spring. A month before the wedding she found out that he was having an affair with his married co-worker. In pain and loss, Jenny scrabbled in the darkness to find love. And the dark found her.

Her third partner, a businessman, charmed the birds from the trees. He was attentive to Michael and Paul and he wanted marriage and kids, just like her (or so he told Jenny). Until she fell pregnant. He gave her an ultimatum: him or the baby.

When she chose her baby, he left. She thought for good, until a month after John was born and the gates of hell opened on her. He wanted control. He wanted his property back: John. He had used her until she was useless, then when she failed to obey him, he dominated and abused her by, what he believed, would hurt her the most. He rained down legal letters on her threatening to take John. It was nothing more than financial and legal rape.

Jenny had to re-mortgage the house. When the judge ruled that he couldn't have sole custody only supervised visits, he took matters into his own hands, and breaking into the house in the middle of the night he attempted to abduct John. John was only two.

It was Michael that had caught him trying to strangle his mum, in her bed. It was Michael who called and later testified to the police against the man he thought would become his father. It was Michael who helped his mum keep the family safe.

They moved to a safe house and eventually relocated far away from Jenny's family. They lost the house but they were together. The businessman deemed he had asserted his authority, taken everything of primary importance (money and security) and not wanting to risk his reputation for the sake of a child he had no interest in, he shrugged his shoulders at his suspended sentence and walked away. For now.

Michael and his mum were always worried that one day he would come back. Michael sometimes confided in Paul, even though Paul didn't really remember much, apart from once having a house filled with lots of toys. John, of course, remembered nothing, and his family circled round him, protecting him and keeping it that way. John was safe, he was protected and he was loved.

Jenny vowed that never again would she trust a man. Her world was her boys and she knew she was lucky they were all alive.

* * *

On the morning of Christmas Eve there was a loud knock at the door. The first smell of trouble was that it was the front door and not the back. Friends always came to the back.

As per usual Jenny looked out of the front

window before answering the door. It was her boss.

The boys stayed in the living room while she went through to the hall. They could hear raised voices. Michael stood up bravely and went through to the hall. Soon after the door slammed and Michael escorted his mum, who was in tears, back through to the living room.

'What's up Mum?' asked John distressed. 'What's happened?'

Michael looked angry and knitted his brows together. 'Mum's boss said he can't pay her this week due to complications working out her overtime. He's going to pay her after Christmas.'

The air in the room sank like lead as all of them felt the disappointment. They knew how their mum had been depending on some money to come through to get some last-minute Christmas essentials today.

Michael sat on the sofa with his arm around his mum. Paul pulled John into the hall. 'I know how to make this better. You go and I'll stay and try and sort this.'

'Go where?' asked John.

'The supermarket. Get a frozen chicken and a Christmas cake. I know where Michael's money is hidden. Come on.' and he motioned John upstairs.

* * *

John felt pretty important on his quest. He was the

one that was going to make it better. Santa had promised they would have a roast for Christmas lunch and he felt like he had Santa on his side, walking with him as he went to make good on that promise.

The supermarket was already very busy. John had the money tucked tight in his pocket and he kept touching it with his hand to make sure it was still there.

Some of the Christmas displays were starting to look tattered and empty as the last of the shoppers made their final purchases. John tried not to gaze too long at all the good things to eat. He had an important job to do.

He went over to the cool cabinet, which was almost completely empty! John stopped in shock for a moment. He hadn't seen it this bad before. Everyone had been panic buying meat before Christmas. There were a few chicken thighs but no whole chickens, or turkeys, or any other type of bird. It was almost apocalyptic.

In panic he ran round the side of the aisle to the freezer chest cabinets, where the frozen birds were usually kept. His feet were like lead as he tried to move. In slow motion he watched a man open the slider of the chest cabinet, reach down and remove the last frozen chicken in the supermarket.

'No. No. Please sir. I need that for my mum.' John managed to squeak. The man turned around in surprise. John tried again. 'Please sir. It's for our Christmas lunch.' John was starting to feel a little teary. 'Please sir. I need that for my mum.' he said again.

Just then Ella from school came up and pointing at John said, 'He's the one who threw the stones at the train Dad.'

John watched the man's face morph red in contrast to his blonde hair, and with a voice as cold as ice he said, 'Well unfortunately we need this chicken for our Boxing Day lunch. You're lucky I didn't report you to the police. Now scram.'

And scram John did. Hot tears flooding down his face. He ran out of the supermarket, along the road, past the fire station and on into the paddocks behind a scrap yard. The back of his right hand was bleeding from where he had caught it on something, he didn't remember when. He sobbed heavily, his little chest heaved in and out. Hot, heavy tears plopped onto his polyester, puffer coat. The world was so unfair.

* * *

Mr Iain Gently and his daughter Ella left the supermarket. Iain was cross. He dragged Ella along as he stomped his way to the car, muttering under his breath, 'Need to learn a lesson . . . Hard school of life . . . Time to grow up and learn what life is about . . . I had it tough . . .' (only Iain hadn't had it tough growing up, comparatively). Iain was so engrossed with his justifications of his poor behaviour that he didn't see the cardboard box someone had left in the carpark.

He went flying. The shopping bags spilled over. The frozen chicken rolled out.

'Oh Dad!' Ella cried out and rushed to help her father. She inspected his grazed hands and retrieved his glasses; the arm on one side was a little wonky.

'I'm fine love, I'm fine.' Iain picked up the shopping and placed the small, frozen chicken back in the bag. It was cold and heavy. Iain was glad to get home after that. He wasn't feeling very good at all.

* * *

When John had stopped crying, he dragged his feet slowly home. Michael's hard-earned money burning a hole in his pocket.

John told his mum and his brothers what had happened. When he got to the last frozen chicken, he started crying all over again. John's mum and brothers hugged him and wiped away the tears. They told him not to worry. John felt like it couldn't get much worse.

Bravely Michael said, 'To be honest I've always thought that tinned spam with gravy tastes just as nice as chicken.' Three sets of sad eyes turned to Michael with hope. Michael put his arm around John and said, 'Let's go back to the supermarket together and see what we can find, eh?' John was proud to have a brother like Michael.

As they went through to the hall and Michael pulled his coat off the coat hook, he caught the hall mirror. Coming off its hook, it deftly slid down along the wall and landed heavily on the protruding plug socket below, before shattering into a million pieces.

No one wanted to say it. They all knew the saying, "Seven years bad luck."

Mustering confidence and strength he didn't know he had Michael turned to his mum, 'Sorry Mum.' Everyone was a little shaken and fractured by the tough time they'd had lately.

Jenny turned to her son with nothing but love. Kissing him on the top of his head she said, 'It's just a mirror. Things can get fixed. Thank God it wasn't one of you.'

Paul grabbed the dustpan and brush from the kitchen. Michael held John back as they tided the glass off the floor. The plug socket had cracked too.

'I'll pop by the hardware store Mum.' said Michael with a confidence that they all clung to. 'You never know what might be in the reduced section.'

His mum hugged him and then topped up the zip on John's coat. 'Lucky things always seem to happen at the right time. Have a look. You never know.' she said.

The boys group hugged Jenny. Whatever life threw at them, they would get through it as a family.

* * *

Iain Gently and his daughter Ella walked along the pavement of the housing estate. The frozen chicken was a heavy weight in the plastic bag that he held.

Santa and his reindeer had attacked most of the houses on the estate and in some places each other, as plastic recreations of them hung from rooves or lay fallen in gardens. Iain watched an old lady trying to right her garden Santa's sleigh, as she balanced precariously on her stick. He counted along the numbers as the old lady turned to watch him walk by.

Number fifty-nine. This was it. Iain purposefully pushed back the garden gate, as paint flaked off in his hands and the cold steel bit back at him. The concrete path was cracked and the grass lay still and long, with frost forming on it as the afternoon air started to chill. Little icicle lights ran round the guttering and he could see a Christmas tree with dancing multi-coloured lights and baubles peeking out from the front, living room window.

Iain knocked on the door. He had the strangest feeling of being watched and turned to see the old lady he'd passed two doors back leaning on her wall, watching them. He felt like a stage actor at the theatre and she was waiting to be amused.

Ella tugged at her dad's hand. 'Daddy . . .' she whispered to him.

'Shh.' he said, as he squeezed her hand a little tighter.

The door opened. There, in the warm glow of

the hall light, stood a woman surrounded by three young boys. She had porcelain-white skin, striking hazel eyes rimmed red (probably from alcohol) and the most extraordinary orange hair. In her hand she held a screwdriver and behind her he could see the remnants of a plug socket on the floor.

'Err . . .' he said, trying to take it all in. The youngest boy, the boy from the supermarket that morning, was looking at him with horror and fear.

'Err . . .' Iain continued. 'I think there was a mistake about a chicken this morning.' he said, offering her the heavy plastic bag in his hand.

Her look cooled.

Iain scrabbled to fill the silence. 'You know you really ought to be careful with that.' he said gesturing at the plug socket. 'Do you want me to do it for you?'

Her look hardened as she replied in an even voice, 'No thank you. I know how to isolate the sockets; they are on a different circuit to the main lights.' She used the screwdriver in her hand to prod upwards in the direction of the hall light above her. 'I don't need your help.' Then she looked angry and put her arm around John. 'John told me about your behaviour regarding the chicken this morning —' Then she swore at him and slammed the door in his face.

Ella jerked Iain's arm as she jumped backwards. From a little distance away, Iain could hear someone laughing.

'Hahahaha! Hohohoho!'

Iain turned to see the old lady he'd passed earlier, near bent over with laughter.

'I'm sorry?' he said. 'What has this got to do with you?'

The old lady continued to laugh as she said, 'Seems like she doesn't need your type of charity, doesn't it? Perhaps it's time to take your patronising charity back to where it came from.' Then the old lady swore at him too. And turning on her heel she and her stick clopped back into her little house, while her body still wobbled with laughter at the man.

* * *

Iain's day had gone from bad to worse. He'd already felt rubbish after the incident with the frozen chicken. He'd tried to make it right and all that happened was he been sworn at. Almost like he was in the wrong!

Iain was distracted through the carol service. He was distant over dinner with Ella. He spent the night tossing and turning dreaming of frozen chickens falling on his head. In all of his dreams he was in the wrong. He had done something wrong.

Iain woke suddenly in the middle of the night, sweating and twisted in his sheets. He exclaimed to the darkness, 'I know what to do! I have a plan!'

The darkness returned silence back to him.

Iain rolled over and fell back to sleep.

* * *

John snugged up to his mum as she opened the large, homemade "envelope" that contained his Christmas present to her. He watched her undo the ribbon at the side to reveal a picture of a steam train. He'd drawn it all himself. He'd coloured it carefully. Blue of course. He'd drawn the driver in (to look a little bit like himself). He'd even attempted the steam and smoke coming out of the steam engine in the right places.

'Oh John!' his mum exclaimed. 'Oh John. This is beautiful.' She held the picture up admiringly. 'I think it is the best picture you have ever drawn. It's stunning my love.' Michael and Paul crowded onto the sofa to look at the picture too, as Jenny held it up, so they could all see. Then she kissed John on the top of his head.

Slowly standing up she said, 'I know just what to do with this.' She went over to the wall above the telly and reaching towards one of the clip frames, reached up, removed her college certificate from the frame and replaced it with John's picture. She then proudly re-placed the clip frame with the train picture, back on the wall.

Turning back to John she said, 'It's a beautiful picture. Thank you.'

All the boys looked pleased.

There was a knock at the front door. Internally they all groaned. Jenny went to the window and peered out, then circling back round to the hall she said, 'It's the little girl from yesterday.'

Opening the door, Ella stood in the doorway, alone.

'Please Miss,' she said. 'My dad's hurt and the ambulance can't come for two hours; can you help me?' She had practiced her lines several times. There was a Polly Pocket Rainbow Funland riding on this.

Jenny looked at the little girl. In her she saw herself. How often had she been scared, or unsure, or needed help?

'Of course I can sweetheart.' she said kindly. 'Boys!' she shouted behind her. 'We need to pop out a minute. Michael, can you turn the oven off and lock the back door? Quickly please.' Paul and John grabbed their coats and wellies. Michael disappeared into the back of the house.

Ella looked up at the lady as she stepped outside. 'You'll need your coat Miss.'

'It's ok.' Jenny said, placing her hand on the young girl's shoulder. 'I don't feel the cold.' She turned to lock the front door behind them all.

John put his cold hand inside his mum's warm one and she gave it a reassuring squeeze as they rushed off along the pavement together.

* * *

Ella's house was very large. John had seen large houses before but he couldn't remember being allowed up the driveway of one. The garden was neat and tidy. Little, grey, gravel stones crunched under his feet. He felt worried but his mum seemed confident, despite her hand being ice cold.

As they entered the house, they quickly removed their shoes and boots. Jenny asked Ella, 'Where is he?'

'Through here . . .' Ella pointed sheepishly.

Jenny rushed through to the kitchen to see Iain Gently, perfectly heathy, basting the most enormous turkey, as the heat of the oven puffed turkey scents and warmth around the cold, hungry family.

John stood behind his mum observing, what seemed to be, something akin to Christmas lunch heaven. His tummy grumbled and his mouth watered at the sights and smells before him - despite it being the mean man hovering over the turkey. Even Michael didn't have any brave or wise words to say as all three boys stood staring and speechless.

'I was hoping you would share our Christmas lunch with us.' Iain said in his nicest, kindest voice.

Before anyone could answer John tugged his mum's hand, and with eyes as wide as saucers he said, 'Oh can we Mum? Can we?' he didn't think he'd smelt something so delicious for practically the whole of his life. There was also a small awareness, somewhere in John's heart, that the man was trying to say sorry for being so mean.

All of Jenny's boys turned to her with hope. Jenny was proud but she wasn't prideful. She knew what this meant to them and if it meant she had to be a little humble for an hour or two then she would.

'That's very kind of you.' she answered slowly. 'Thank you very much, we'd love to join you.'

Everybody relaxed. The boys let out a little cheer and allowed themselves to audibly sniff the air and say, "Yumm."

Iain beamed with pleasure. Ella stood back a little, watching and trying to work out what was going on. She knew her dad had done something wrong and that he was trying to make it right. Her job was to be a polite hostess as he'd instructed her.

Iain continued, 'Lunch should be ready in about forty minutes.' he said. 'Perhaps you'd like to watch a movie together while I finish preparing it?'

John couldn't believe how his Christmas was panning out. He didn't exactly like or trust the man, but he had turkey and . . . 'Can we watch the *Polar Express* please?' he asked with excitement.

Iain turned to John with raised eyebrows. 'So you like trains do you?'

'More than anything in the world!' John exclaimed, then quickly added, 'Except Mum.' loyally holding her hand.

Iain carefully closed the oven door behind the turkey and gave his full attention to the young boy.

'I do too.' he said simply. In that moment man and boy connected in a kindred love of trains. 'I have a Hornby train set I've been working on in the attic. Do you want to see it?'

John could not possibly believe the day could get any better. He turned to his mum.

'Well . . .' she said, thinking they knew very little about this man and what they did know hadn't been overwhelmingly favourable so far.

John begged her, 'Please Mum. Please. Please.'

Jenny caved. 'Very well. We are just here if you need anything.' She turned to Iain, carefully watching him. 'Do you want me to help with the lunch preparations?'

'Yes.' Iain said graciously, 'Thank you.'

Ella wasn't that fond of trains, but she knew she had to be a good hostess; her dad had told her so. Besides she knew Paul and John from school, so she suggested showing them round then starting the DVD ready for when her dad and John came back down from the attic. Jenny donned a spare apron as her children scattered. Iain led the way to the attic.

The sight that met John was something he could never have dreamt of. Over the entirety of the attic space of the house was a large, MDF table with walking space round the edge. On it, part constructed, was the most extensive train set he'd ever seen. Little stacks of tracks lay in bundles, in various places, waiting to be placed. Some of the trains and trailers had been arranged side by side, ready to go, almost as if they we surrounded by an investable shed. There were stations and people, farms and trees, all in the process of being unpacked.

'Oh wow!' said John impressed. He never knew something like this existed. This man must be very, very rich. He cautiously went over to one of the trains and peered down to look at it.

'You can pick it up if you like.' Iain said graciously.

As if he was holding a delicate, porcelain cup John gently picked up the train and studied it. He knew all the components and names of the different parts of the train by heart. He'd read books from the library. He knew the famous trains like: *The Mallard, City of Truro, Stephenson's Rocket and The Flying Scotsman.*

Iain spied one of his unused Hornby train sets in the corner. It was a Christmas novelty set – although of Hornby quality. It had a fluorescent yellow label with ninety pounds crossed out and forty-five pounds written over it. He'd picked it up from a car boot sale last summer. Unobserved he picked the label off while John admired the trains on display, then dusting off the box with his hands he offered it to John.

It was quite possibly the best present John had ever received. All he could keep saying was, 'Wow.' and 'Thank you.'

Iain felt wonderful, not only because John was happy and he'd done something nice for him rather than making him cry, but also because he could see in John the niche enthusiasm for trains that Iain had had his whole life.

When Iain and John returned downstairs, they found Ella, Paul and Michael happily snugged up in the TV room watching Christmas films, and Jenny in the kitchen where she'd nearly finished serving up lunch.

John knew his mum wouldn't grumble being left to sort lunch. She never did. She often said it made her happy to do things for other people. He also knew that everyone was looking forward to the turkey.

* * *

Lunch was delicious and it was happy. Everyone relaxed and unwound. Ella found she quite liked having other people to talk to. Jenny was happy that her boys were happy. Iain was glad to have finally found a way to be acceptably kind and not condescending. And John? John felt as if this was the best day of his life and he never wanted it to end.

As they tidied up after lunch and John's mum started to make comments about getting back, John tried to delay things a little.

'Mum, Mr Gently said he has a piano. Didn't you used to play a piano Mum?'

Iain looked at Jenny and her strange orange hair in surprise. He offered, 'You are more than welcome to play. It was my mother's but neither of us play. I still keep it tuned though.'

John thought it was strange to have a piano

when you didn't play it, but he kept his thoughts to himself, as his mum allowed herself to be led through to the formal sitting room.

John watched her tentatively run her hands along the wood of the baby grand. He watched her slowly sit down and stretch out her bony, hard-working fingers. John had never heard his mum play but Michael sometimes mentioned it. As Jenny's hands stretched in recognition, she started playing.

It was completely different, like nothing John had ever heard before. He stood there, clutching his train set box, watching his mum. John was not the only person transfixed by his mum's talent. Iain similarly stood transfixed by this remarkable woman. Paul and Michael crowded around her. Ella wished she could be her.

When she finished Jenny smiled contentedly. She'd loved her piano. Yes, she'd missed this. But obviously her boys were so much more important. One day she'd pick up a second-hand piano. One day.

John broke the silence, 'What was that mum? What was that music?'

She turned and smiled to him, '*The Heart Asks Pleasure First*. It's by Michael Nyman. One of my favourites. Well!' she said closing the lid on the piano. 'Time to go.'

At the front door, as they were putting on their boots, John watched Iain give Jenny his mobile number. John was really glad. It meant he could come back and see the trains.

The family walked back home in the cooling afternoon with many mixed emotions. John asked, 'Mum. Are we going to see him again?'

Jenny squeezed his hand a little tighter. 'We've had such a lovely day, haven't we? But, my love, you can never trust a man completely. One act of kindness, or even two or three acts of kindness doesn't a kind man make. It takes time to learn someone's true character. And you are all too important to me to risk anyone hurting any of you ever again.'

John had a feeling that he probably shouldn't talk about the subject again, so he just hugged his train set a little tighter. Realising, as he did so, that all of the things he'd asked for from Santa, apart from the ride on the steam train, had come true.

* * *

In the spring came John's birthday and with it a few more freedoms. He was allowed to go to the library by himself, if he said what time he was coming back by. And now that his mum had a new job, she set all the boys little errands and jobs to do each week, to allow them to earn a little pocket money for sweets. John was allowed to go to the sweetshop alone too. The sweetshop was on the same street as the old train station.

John would always add ten minutes to his allotted time on a Saturday morning, so he had time to peer in each of the gates around the station and see which of the steam locomotives the volunteer engineers were working on this week. On Sundays they would allow visitors onto the trains and they would run the steam engines up and down the restored track to the next nearest town.

John pressed his face to the steel bars of the main gateway into the engineering yard. There was a big yellow crane lifting blue sacks from the ground onto a railway trailer. Several men in orange suits hung around talking or directing or watching. John wondered what they were doing. One of the men turned around and John instinctively recognised Mr Gently. He waved and Iain waved back and came over.

'Hello John.' he said, and recognising the same glint in the young boy's eye that was in his own, he offered, 'Do you want to come in?'

'Yes please!' And forgetting all about, "being back in twenty minutes" he followed Iain Gently into the yard. 'Where's Ella?' John asked, looking around.

'Oh she's with her mum.' Iain replied.

John knew about these things, except that he didn't see his dad. He knew that he'd been to prison for trying to hurt them all – or something like that. John shuddered at the thought. They were quite happy just as they were.

Iain showed John around and explained about different parts of the trains. One of the steam trains was being fired up.

'We're going to give this one a run out before the visitors come tomorrow. Would you like to come?'

John didn't hesitate, of course it was a, "Yes." he didn't even consider his mum.

* * *

Iain Gently helped John up into the cab of the train. The driver smiled kindly at John as he directed John where to stand. Holding on, as instructed, John watched the men get to work; opening the furnace and loading it with coal, playing with the levers and working with their colleagues to get clearance to leave the station.

Then they were off! The engine sounded like a huge rumbling dragon with steam snorting out. Slowly they built speed as the massive engine moved out of the station, gathering pace, under the bridge where John had stood watching so many times, past the signals, out into the countryside.

It felt like they were flying along. The distinctive smoke and steam smell from the engine filled John's nostrils. The men monitored the dials and levers, they were covered in dirt and grease, but they didn't care. John clutched his sweets, his eyes wide open and his heart thumping in time with the engine. It was wonderful.

* * *

It was only when they got back to the station again, an hour later, that John remembered his promise to his mum.

Iain told him not to worry and gave John's mum a call on his mobile. John could hear a heated discussion over the phone. Mr Gently then hung up and said, 'Look, I'd better walk you back home. Is that ok?'

'Am I in trouble?' John asked.

'Nope, I think I'm in trouble.' said Iain, and sighed a little bit.

As they walked along the pavement, Iain in his dirty, orange boiler suit and John clutching his sweets, John wondered what his mum would say. He definitely wouldn't be allowed to go on the train again. He was gutted.

As they passed by Mrs Horrel's garden she hobbled out on her stick.

'Hello Mrs Horrel!' John called.

'Hello!' she waved back.

'Good morning.' Iain offered, wondering what she was coming out to see this time.

Almost as if she'd read his mind she quipped, 'Just positioning myself ready for the morning's entertainment!' and winking again at John (he preferred the winks to the hair ruffles) she leant her elbows on the garden wall and watched them up the path to the front door of number fifty-nine.

John's mum looked a little out of sorts and asked Iain inside. 'John, you go and sit in the living room while I talk to Mr Gently.' she instructed. 'I also think you owe your brothers an apology, as they have been out looking for you this morning.'

John felt pretty bad. He had been so excited about the train he just hadn't thought about it. He apologised to his brothers and to make up for it he offered to share his sweets.

All three boys sat on the sofa, in the quiet, sucking gobstoppers, trying to hear what their mum was saying in the kitchen. After what seemed like quite a long time, their mum came out and into the living room with Iain.

'John,' she said as she knelt in front of him. 'I know you love trains, but what you did today was really, really dangerous. Mummy was worried somebody bad had taken you.' Paul and Michael exchanged looks over John's head. Jenny continued, 'It is ok to sometimes go and play at Mr Gently's house with his trains and to go on the steam train with him, but, it needs to be prearranged and you have to promise to stick to the times we have agreed. Does that sound ok?'

John was so happy. He thought he was going to get grounded, he thought he would never get to go on the steam train again. Instead, he was going to be able to play with Mr Gently's train set and he would get to go to see the steam trains. John was happy to agree to any terms under those circumstances.

John watched his mum escort Mr Gently to the front door.

At the doorstep Iain smiled at Jenny and said,

'Thank you. I'm glad you understand. I know how he feels as I was exactly the same at his age.'

Jenny replied, 'I'm just glad he is safe and happy. That's all that matters.'

As Iain walked back down the pavement, out of the housing estate, he still had a silly smile on his face, until Mrs Horrel called out to him:

'Ahh, the lovely Jenny, well worth the courting! But you're going to have to put in a bit more effort than that!' and chuckling she wobbled off back indoors, her black walking stick clopping along the path beside her.

* * *

It was Christmas Eve and many things had changed since the last Christmas.

The first change was their mum had got a better job. Her boss was nice and she was able to buy presents and put them under the tree before Christmas; so the boys knew they were there and that they were going to get something this year. Also, they didn't have to worry about the turkey, as they were going to eat with Mr Gently and Ella again, and John knew for a fact that Mr Gently had a turkey, as he had shown John when he went over to play with the Hornby trains on Wednesday afternoon.

Every Wednesday John went to Mr Gently's house to play trains, and every Saturday morning he was allowed to visit the train yard. And if the steam train was out on the Saturday, John was quite often allowed to go in the cab with the driver for a ride out.

John's knowledge of trains had increased rapidly and he loved to get train books from the library; he was ever hungry to learn more. Mr Gently had even recommended a few books and John had been able to make a library request for them.

John had had a wonderful year. When it came to writing a letter to Santa at the start of December John didn't know what to put, as he already had everything he wanted. Some of the kids in his school year said Santa didn't exist, but John knew better. He'd got everything he'd asked for.

It was strange that he'd once been so upset and scared by Mr Gently, whereas now he couldn't imagine not having this kind, interesting man around. Mr Gently knew so much about trains. John was also aware that his mum wasn't angry at Mr Gently anymore, which was a relief.

John hadn't said anything to his brothers, because they'd been out at the time, but one Saturday, a couple of weeks ago, when Mr Gently had walked John back home, something had happened.

Mr Gently had taken his boots off at the back door to have a cup of tea with John's mum. John had gone upstairs to add some track that Mr Gently had given him, to his track for his *Polar Express* (as John liked to call his Hornby Christmas train). When John had come back down to the kitchen he'd seen his mum pass Mr Gently his tea, and he watched Mr Gently put it down on the kitchen work surface, then he'd reached forward and taking John's mum's hand, he pulled her towards him and kissed her. John thought his mum was going to be angry but she wasn't. John felt a bit awkward watching, so he quietly went back upstairs to play with his train.

Anyway, John reasoned. If his mum and Mr Gently did get married then he could get to play with Mr Gently's trains all the time. Besides Ella already called him and Paul her brothers at school, Paul had even sorted out one of the girls that had been bullying her in her class. They were pretty much family anyway and families were always better bigger.

John and his brothers went to sleep that Christmas Eve imagining what surprises Christmas Day might bring this year. They all had a good feeling about it.

Michael imagined what it would be like not to have to be responsible all the time and what it might be like to feel safe and protected again. Paul liked being a big brother, he admired Michael and wanted to be just like him. He liked it when Ella asked for his help and called him her big brother, just as John did. John imagined being on a steam train . . . it was the *Polar Express* . . . the train jostled and jiggled as it left the station . . . the little girl next to him, who looked a little like Ella, but not quite, said that Santa was going to be on board and had he thought of what he was going to ask Santa for? . . . John drifted off to sleep.

8. UNDER THE MISTLETOE

Sarah sipped from her warm mug of hot chocolate. It was snowing outside and her hair was still wet from the shower.

The clock on the mantlepiece read seven-thirty p.m. She should have been dressed by now. She should have had her hair dried and styled. But inside she really couldn't be bothered. "What is it all for?" she asked herself.

The red, party dress hung from the wardrobe door. When Sarah bought it she imagined the fun she would be having wearing it, she imagined how pretty she would look, and somewhere, very deep down inside, she imagined someone special noticing her, their eyes meeting across a crowded room, a romantic kiss and . . . happily ever after.

'It's not happened yet; it's not going to happen.' She despondently said to the empty room, as she slumped down on the sofa and switched the TV on. In her hands she clutched the warm mug a little tighter.

* * *

'Dave? Dave?' Bernice shouted across the flat. 'Where have you been? People are due in half an hour. I'm surprised someone hasn't shown up early already, and you're not even showered or dressed. I've had to put all the party food out by myself. I've only just had time to get ready!' Bernice ran out of things to say.

Dave stood in the hall, muffled against the snow outside and admired his beautiful wife. He could never be cross, firstly because he loved her and secondly because she was right. He knew she'd forgive him though, especially when she saw . . .

'And what have you got in your hand?' she grumbled.

Dave held aloft the large, brown paper bag and waved it at her. 'I have a surprise for the party!' Bernice rolled her eyes. 'Want a kiss?' he said, trying to wrap his arm around her.

'No, you're all wet from the snow, I've just done my makeup, you're ruining my dress.' Bernice pushed him away.

Dave's eyes sparkled as he said, 'Want to look inside?' He knew her better than she knew herself. Unable to stay her curiosity she peered inside and gave a squeal of delight. Dave handed her the bag as he peeled off his damp coat and scarf.

'Do you want a kiss?' he said softly, wrapping his arms around her again. Bernice took the mistletoe out of the bag and held it over their heads.

* * *

Rupert peered through the damp snow flurry. He'd decided to walk. His shoes were wet and he was worried the snow had messed up the gel in his hair. Dirty-white sludge draped over the sign announcing: Paradise Road.

"That's the one." he thought, trudging along the road in the tracks made by the cars. Inside a little voice said, "Is this really worth it?" Rupert pulled up his coat collar and trudged on.

* * *

The taxi pulled up to the flats.

'Oh thank you so much. And I really do appreciate you coming at such short notice.' said Sarah.

'That's alright love.' the taxi driver replied. 'You were lucky, I had a last-minute cancellation.'

'Serendipity.' Sarah said, almost to herself.

'Everything happens for a reason.' He turned around and looked at her. 'Every step you have taken has led you to this moment.' Sarah felt as though she had been struck by lightning. The taxi driver winked and said, 'That's eight pounds fifty.' as he reset his machine.

Absentmindedly Sarah fished ten pounds out of her purse and handed it to the taxi driver. 'Please keep the change.' she said on autopilot.

Sarah delicately stepped out of the car in her strappy heels, onto the snowy pavement. The cold on her feet bought her back to the moment, as the taxi driver called, 'Don't forget to book your return. It's busy tonight love.'

She smiled back into the cab as she said, 'Thank you so much. I won't.' and shut the door.

Wet, sleety-snow whirled around the taxi as the tail lights disappeared into the night. It was cold! Sarah pulled up the collar on her coat and delicately balance beamed her way to the communal front door. Her red-gloved hand pressed the buzzer, and Bernice's cheerful voice jumped out into the darkness.

'Hellooo!' It sounded as if things were already in full swing. Bernice sounded merry.

'It's Sarah.'

'Come on up! Second floor on the right.'

'*Buzz.*' The door clicked open. Using both hands Sarah pulled the heavy door back and wobbled through in her red, strappy heels. "Ok, not such a practical decision tonight." She thought as she started to mount the stairs.

* * *

'I can't go back now.' Rupert thought as he was buzzed on through. Inside the shared hallway it was warm and bright. The most delicious scent wafted around him. Like a sniffer dog on a trail, he followed it all the way up the flights of stairs. It reminded him of vanilla, hot chocolate and sweet-smelling flowers. He couldn't put his finger on it but it was absolutely delightful. He happily inhaled the air as he reached the second floor.

There, in front of him, waiting where he wanted to go, was a stunning brunette, wrapped up in a red coat with the most ridiculously wonderful, strappy, heeled, red shoes. She turned to look at him. Her eyelashes fluttered over pretty, blue eyes as she spoke.

'Are you here for the party too?' she asked. Sarah took in his deep-brown eyes and lightly tanned skin. His brown wavy hair appeared to have been savaged by the weather and snow was melting in it.

The words stuck in his throat. All he could think about was his damp shoes and messed up hair. He tried to smooth his coat as he replied, 'Yes! What a night.' He turned his head to indicate the snow outside. His voice sounded high and strained.

Bernice burst through the front door. 'How wonderful to see you!' she said to Sarah. Then noticing Rupert, she said, 'I didn't know you knew each other.'

'No, we've just met.' replied Sarah. Rupert tried not to look at Sarah, he felt like he was a rabbit in the headlights.

'Do come in!' Bernice wafted them through the door and took their coats. Sarah looked stunning in a cherry-red, classic-cut, satin dress. Rupert felt like the biggest loser in the world and he had damp shoes. Bernice bunded their coats up together to fling them on the guest bed. With a twinkle in her eye she said, 'Dave's in the kitchen serving drinks, do go through, after, of course, you have kissed under the mistletoe.'

Both looked up in horror at the bomb above them. Rupert turned bright red and Sarah said sharply, 'Sorry, I don't do kissing.'

As soon as she said it, she regretted it. Bernice laughed it off and Rupert followed Sarah through to the kitchen.

* * *

Sarah felt rude. She didn't mean to say it quite like that. She twisted her hands uncomfortably as she sat in the corner, talking to a very boring friend of Dave's. Mark, Dave's friend, obviously thought he was winning. He completely misread the signs of boredom and incompatibility, so he ploughed on. Sarah wished the ground would swallow her up. She knew she shouldn't have come.

Sarah looked around the room. A Christmas tree sparkled in the corner: warm, fairy lights, twinkling their magic. Little presents were wrapped in gold ribbon under the tree. There were perhaps twenty guests dotted about. Some guests were around the nibbles adorning the Christmas-decorated dining table. Some were vying for the role of DJ of the year near the music. They all looked so happy. So *together.* Sarah wished she wasn't here, but more than that she wished she hadn't been rude. She desperately wanted to apologise.

She scanned the room for Rupert. At that very moment Rupert turned around from the group he was talking with and their eyes locked across the busy room. Electricity zipped through her spine as her eyes drank in the deep-brown colour of his. He looked away quickly. Sarah felt her cheeks melt red.

* * *

Finally, Sarah managed to extract herself from Mark's onslaught. He tried to follow her until she politely, but firmly, said she had to go to the bathroom.

The bathroom was cool. Sarah steadied herself against the sink. Perhaps she'd had more to drink than she realised? It was that awful man. She felt her skin recoil at the thought. Ugh. She felt icky just thinking about him.

Sarah retouched her makeup, straightened her dress and took a deep breath. One last try to apologise and then she would leave.

* * *

Rupert took another glug of whisky. He'd probably had too much. Inside he winced. He'd just met the most impossibly beautiful woman of his life and the last person she would ever consider kissing was him.

Someone had started a classic Christmas mix of songs. Mariah Carey's 'All I Want For Christmas Is You' jingled through the room. Rupert thought he could smell wet puppies – was that his feet? In embarrassment he left the group he was talking with and headed to the kitchen for a top up. He nearly collided headlong into Sarah. The scent of her stunned him. It was like walking into a beautiful, soft-scented cloud.

'I'm sorry.' he spluttered, as he just managed to stop himself pouring the last of his whisky over her cherry-red, satin dress. Their eyes locked.

'No, not at all.' she replied. Inside she said to herself, "Say it, say it now – I'm sorry – say it."

'Top up.' Rupert said, waving his glass between them and ducked into the kitchen.

Sarah turned to his back. Mariah sang eternal Christmas love over the airwaves – one soulmate for Christmas. "That's it!" Sarah thought. "I knew it was a mistake to come." Sarah made her excuses to a very exuberant Bernice, who had definitely had more than a couple of drinks. As Sarah turned to leave the room she grimaced slightly as she saw Mark cornering another poor target; she was trying to crawl backwards up the wall away from his alcohol breath and him. Ugh – poor thing.

Sarah sorted through the coats on the guest bed in the spare bedroom. Wrapped up with hers was a blue, wool, man's coat, damp with the snow and the sleet. As she touched it she was transported back to the start of the evening, the moment she saw his beautiful deep-brown eyes, lightly tanned skin and toned jaw. But not for her, apparently. Perhaps she was fated to be alone? A little sigh escaped her lips and her heart dipped as she put on her cold, damp coat. Bother, she remembered, she hadn't ordered a taxi back.

* * *

As Rupert entered the kitchen his brain caught up with his actions. She didn't have a drink in her hands. Perhaps, he should just try. "She's not interested" his fears mocked him. "Just try" his ego answered back. Perhaps if they could just talk, then she wouldn't find him so repulsive. Every time he was close to her he felt the pull. His pride rose within him. He wasn't that bad! Boldly he grabbed two glasses of champagne. He returned to the party but scanning around he couldn't see a red dress in sight. Where was she?

* * *

Sarah stood in the hall and googled another taxi company. How embarrassing. She didn't want to return to her hosts just after she had said her goodbyes. The sleety-snow outside smeared itself against the bedroom windows. It looked cold out. She shuddered and turned back to her phone.

A voice behind her said, 'I thought we should say

"hello" properly. Champagne?'

Sarah turned to a pair of lovely warm, deep-brown eyes. She felt the magnetism of them draw her to him.

'I, er, um, I was about to go actually.' she shook her phone. 'Taxis!' she exclaimed in a mock cheerful manner and rolled her eyes.

'Oh.' said Rupert a little deflated.

Her conscience bit at her: "Now is your chance Sarah. Thaw a little." Trying her best smile, Sarah said, 'Oh, well, a little sip won't hurt.' She graciously accepted the glass from Rupert. The party in the room behind them was noisy and busy. But here in the hallway, it was quiet, warm and comfortable.

'I have a taxi booked for a little later.' said Rupert. 'You could share with me if you like?' He stopped suddenly, perhaps he had gone too far.

'You do?' said Sarah hopefully.

'Of course.' he replied. Sarah shivered slightly in her damp coat. 'Hey, your coat is damp.' he said. Helping her out of her damp coat their hands briefly touched. He hung the coat on the small stand near the radiator. Just under the mistletoe.

* * *

Dave tapped Bernice on the shoulder. He whispered into her ear. 'You're such a troublesome, little matchmaker, I know you will gloat about being right all over me, but can I just say – I bought the mistletoe.'

Bernice raised an eyebrow to her husband. Exiting the group she was in, she tiptoed over to the doorway with him, and following his lead and shushed lips, she peaked round the corner. There, in the hall, Rupert and Sarah were deep in conversation. Their eyes not breaking for a breath. It was as if they were they only two people in the world. Turning back to her husband she gave him a very knowing and very happy smile. He winked back to her and they re-joined the party.

* * *

The conversation lulled. Rupert's phone buzzed. Apologising, he checked it. 'That's a text from the taxi company. Are you still ok for me to get you back home safely?'

'That's just perfect.' Sarah said, smiling up at him.

Michael Bublé and Idina Menzel sang their duet of 'Baby It's Cold Outside' from the speakers next door in the living room. It felt cosy and warm here, in the hall, with Rupert.

Perhaps it was the champagne, or perhaps the mistletoe above their heads showering down special, little stars of magic, but in that moment Rupert slowly leant his head down to Sarah's and their soft lips connected.

9. SPARKLING SNOWFLAKES AND WEDDING WISHES

Dedicated to Daphne.

Lesley looked at herself in the mirror. As she moved her head from side to side, she watched her straight, blonde, shoulder-length hair, swish and shimmer in the fairy lights that adorned her dressing table. She turned her head and looked at herself from over her shoulder. "Am I beautiful?" she asked herself. She reached her hands up to her face and smoothed out the fine lines that had started to appear around her eyes and over her forehead. "Am I fooling myself?" she asked inside. She let out a deep sigh and tried to let a thousand years of feeling unseen, unwanted and different evaporate away.

Twisting on the stool, Lesley reached down to the bottom drawer of her dressing table and took out a pretty, cardboard box. It was cream-coloured and adorned with spring flowers. "It's ironic," she thought, "that this should come in my autumn years and not my spring." Her one regret was that she'd never had children. But fate had still decreed that she should find happiness. As her mum had once told her, "Everyone deserves their place in the sun."

Mustering the confidence that had been growing within her the last few years, Lesley opened the box. Inside was a delicate, wire-wrapped tiara. Little, sparkling crystals and tiny pearls, dropped from twists of gold wire. It was the perfect accessory for her winter wedding.

Lesley gently removed the tiara from the box and placed it on her head, deftly moving strands of hair to cover the edges. Again, she watched herself in the mirror as she moved her head from side to side.

Was it really her turn? Was she really going to be a bride?

* * *

Lesley was fourteen. Her mum had been out shopping. Lesley was back from school and she was supposed to be doing her homework.

When she was alone in the house it was her favourite secret pastime, to sneak into her parent's bedroom and play dress-up with her mum's things. Lesley put her socked feet into her mum's stilettoes and she practised walking up and down in front of the wardrobe mirror.

Lesley wondered what sort of woman she would be. Alluring? She made a come-hither gesture at herself in the mirror. Sexy? She pushed her chest up and made kissing faces. Plain? She grabbed her mum's church coat and buttoned it up to the neck. All women must hide themselves at some point in their lives. That's how it was for a woman: be beautiful, but don't flaunt yourself; be alluring, but don't do "it"; be intelligent, but keep your opinions to yourself. Lesley wondered who she was inside. Was she the person she could be or the person they wanted her to be?

Dressing-up was one of the small moments in Lesley's life when she felt like she didn't need to hide. She opened the zip on her mum's makeup bag and removed a lipstick. 'Ruby Red.' she read aloud. Shrugging Lesley removed the top and expertly applied the lipstick. She'd seen her mum do it a thousand times; she knew exactly what to do.

'What on earth are you doing?' Lesley's mum shouted. Lesley jumped a full foot in the air. Behind her in the doorway stood her mum just back from shopping. Lesley had been so engrossed that she hadn't heard her mum come home. Her mum continued, 'What if you father came home? What if your father saw you looking like this?' Her mum crossly passed Lesley a tissue to wipe off the red lipstick. Despite appearances Lesley knew her mum wasn't angry at her. Her mum was afraid.

Lesley shuddered to think what *would* happen if her father found her dressed like this. When she was small her father had made it quite clear that he wanted a son, not a daughter.

Lesley pulled off her mum's church coat, while her mum quickly folded and stowed away the other items of clothing. Her mum surveyed the bedroom. They had successfully tidied up. Her mum then ushered Lesley back to her bedroom saying, 'Grab your schoolbooks, come down to the kitchen and do your homework at the table. While I make dinner before your father gets home.'

Without making eye contact her mum gently squeezed Lesley's retreating, drooping shoulders. Lesley turned to see the retreating back of her mum vanishing down the stairs.

* * *

Lesley came back to now. She was boiling the kettle to make tea. Her cousin Hugo had texted to say he had just exited the motorway and stopped for fuel. He estimated he was about five minutes away. Just the right amount of time to let the tea brew.

The last few years had been scary for Lesley. A baptism of fire. Something had changed within her. It was almost as if she could no longer bear to be the person other people wanted her to be anymore. By shedding the layers of other's expectations – like shedding old layers of onion skin – Lesley was starting to find out who she really was inside. She discovered she was able to say, 'I like it.' or 'I don't like it.' without cringing at the recipient's response. She was even brave enough to use the words, 'I want.' and 'I don't want.' She had found the power of: No. Finally, Lesley was learning who she was. And surprisingly, she liked herself.

Lesley was breaking free. For too long she had been cooped up inside herself. As her confidence grew, as she learnt what made her happy and aligned more closely to her authentic self, then she was able to attract to her the one thing that had eluded her all these years: love.

The doorbell rang. Rushing to the door, with excitement and trepidation, Lesley greeted her cousin Hugo. He stepped back in surprise, then tried to cover his response. Lesley knew she looked different. She knew she'd changed both inside and out. And that was ok.

Lesley hugged her cousin. 'It's great to see you.' she said. 'Thanks for coming.'

'Hey,' he said. 'it's important. You're getting married!' He held up a pretty paper bag with silver wedding bells on it.

Lesley giggled like a schoolgirl as she ushered him in. 'Thank you.' she said graciously, as she took the gift from him. She was starting to feel like the blushing bride. Gradually, over the last few years, she had become more and more visible, and recently she felt like she was being *seen.*

Hugo draped his coat over the back of the kitchen chair and sat down. Lesley grabbed some mugs and started pouring out the tea.

'So – ' he said conversationally, 'everything sorted? Any last minute jitters?'

'Everything is sorted. Everything that can be before the day. The cake is still to be decorated Friday, but the cake makers did a beautiful mini example cake with pastel colours and primroses, so I'm not too worried. There are one or two invitations that we haven't had a reply from, but I guess that's to be expected . . .'

'I wouldn't take it personally.' Hugo said, gratefully accepting the hot cup of tea that Lesley passed to him. 'It probably says more about them than you.'

'I know.' she said. 'I'm kind of used to people not being interested or judging when they don't really understand.'

Hugo looked at his cousin. He could feel a lump in his throat. He suddenly felt very sorry for the lonely path Lesley had had to walk up until this point. Lesley noticed his expression change.

'It's ok.' she said. 'Really it's ok. The most important thing is . . . I'm in love.'

He reached over the kitchen table and put his hand over hers. 'I'm really happy for you, for you both. We all are.'

Lesley smiled radiantly back. She had never believed love would find her. All the wonderful things that she'd watch come to other people and now they were coming to her. Her doubt had gone. She was so very happy. But Hugo was wrong. Not everyone was enjoying Lesley's newfound happiness.

* * *

Lesley shivered in the garage. She was supposed to be at an after-school club; she was supposed to be at football practice. It was what her father wanted.

Instead, she was in the unused garage beside her parent's house. It was piled high with boxes, old furniture and cobwebs. It was dark and cold. But she was safe and she was happy.

She'd found an old car blanket in a box, and by the light of a torch she was reading a romantic novel. The title was in bold, pink, italicised script, proclaiming: *The Highway Prince.*

Lesley snacked on some slices of apple her mum had packed in her school bag that morning, as she read:

Holding the pistol aloft he shouted, 'Halt!' and fired a warning shot into the darkness to show he meant business.

The carriage lurched to a halt as the coachman and groom raised their hands. The horses whinnied and shied, trying to move, not wanting to stop.

Guy moved round to the carriage door. He opened it roughly and to his astonishment he saw . . .

'Lesley! What are you doing?' Lesley's mum cried out. Lesley was like a cat with nine lives. It was nearly always her mum that caught her and covered for her. That wasn't by accident. 'What are you doing in the dark all alone? You are supposed to be at football practice.'

Lesley sat frozen still like a statue, caught mid-crime, holding the torch over the incriminating evidence.

Her mum rushed over and snatched the book from her hands. 'Where on earth did you get hold of this?' then she delivered the line that delineated Lesley's childhood years: 'What would your father say if he saw you with *this*. You know how he feels about romance novels.' She shook her head in disbelief, but her eyes betrayed her fear. She repeated, 'Where did you get this from Lesley?' shaking the book at her.

'The public library.' Lesley confessed. She felt her body shrink within her skin at the shame of it. Today she died a little bit more inside.

'Oh Lesley. The public library? How could you be so thoughtless.' Her mum shook her head. 'I'll return it in the morning for you.' With a sudden pang of guilt her voice softened. 'I'm sorry love, I'm only trying to protect you. You know that don't you?'

'Yes.' Lesley mumbled, nodding her head sadly

with disappointment.

As often happened when her mum was trying to do the right thing, she quoted scripture to her. 'The Lord only gives us as much as we can bear.' She paused for a moment, then continued with a teary voice, 'I just don't know how long I can go on protecting you for my love.' She cupped Lesley's face with her hand. They both knew that was a lie. Lesley's mum would never stop protecting her, until her dying breath.

* * *

It was a cold December day. A northerly wind swept past the hotel windows. Inside the hotel it was warm.

Lesley stood in front of the closed double doors and took a deep breath to steady her nerves. This was it. Her new life was just the other side of the doors. In a few moments she would walk through to a life she could only have dreamt of a few years ago. Sometimes she amazed herself at how far she'd come.

To her right stood her good friend Dave. They'd been friends since university. Dave was one of many people who, with the love of a true friend, watched Lesley's morphosis. He looked sideways at her. She looked radiant.

The minister came out from a side door and scuttled over. He put a reassuring hand on Lesley's arm, saying, 'How are you?'

'Yes, good.' Lesley replied a little nervously.

'Ready?' he asked, looking at both Lesley and her friend, and noting delicately that it wasn't her father with her today.

'As ready as I'll ever be!' she said bravely, reaching up to put her arm through Dave's arm, ready to walk down the aisle.

'Wonderful.' The minister beamed. 'I'll ask them to start the music.' The minister disappeared back through the side door.

From the other side of the double doors Lesley heard the music start: 'A Thousand Years'. They had so carefully chosen the song. It represented everything they'd both been through. Lesley took a deep breath and with the support of her friend walked *one step closer* as the doors swung open and she stepped forward.

The guests stood to great her and there was an audible gasp as they really seemed to *see* Lesley for the first time. She saw her cousin Hugo in the crowd. He smiled at her and nodded in approval.

Lesley's dress was a light-pink colour; she had reasoned she wasn't traditional and tradition had been a straitjacket her entire life. This dress reflected who she was. The dress fell in a princess line from the chest. The sweetheart neckline was modestly covered with pink lace up to her shoulders. Entwined in her blonde hair was the feather-light, gold, wire tiara, adorned with little droplets of pearls and crystals, which twinkled under the venue lights. In her hand was a bouquet packed with white roses, to symbolise hope and new beginnings.

Lesley raised her eyes, pricked with tears, and locked them on her soon to be wife who stood before her.

Marie, her rock. How could she have known it could be like this?

Marie's light-grey suit complimented Lesley's light-pink wedding dress perfectly. Marie also had a pink tie and pocket handkerchief. They were a matched pair.

Marie was similarly teary-eyed as she looked at Lesley, her soon to be wife, walking towards her. Beside Marie, on a stand by itself, was a large, white candle. It represented Lesley's mum. Lesley knew if she were alive, she would be here today.

Magic fell on the room, as two people, so very in love, were standing here before them to declare it openly.

Outside it started to gently snow. Snowflakes stuck to the window, clamouring to peer inside, twinkling as they reflected the warm glow of the room.

* * *

In a pub a few miles away, Jeff sat at the poorly lit bar, slumped over a pint of beer. He'd barely touched a drop. The pub was the place he went to, to find solace, now that he was alone.

An old work friend approached the bar and

greeted Jeff, 'Hey Jeff!' he said good-naturedly.

Jeff just about managed a reply.

His friend persevered conversationally, 'Hey, I hear your daughter Lesley is getting married. Congratulations.' he held out his hand.

Jeff looked as if he had been slapped. He stood up abruptly, knocking over the bar stool and announced to the room, 'I don't have a daughter.' He tightened his fists and his face went red, as he shouted in a high-pitched voice, 'I have a son!'

In anger he walked out of the pub into the oncoming weather, letting the door slam behind him in the wind. How could he deny the life they'd led? He wouldn't change the reality he'd chosen for Lesley.

Little specks of snow started to fall and the snowflakes stung his face in the oncoming wind. If you looked closely, they almost looked like tears melting onto his cheeks. The truth was, he did love Lesley, he just wasn't brave enough to let the world see that.

* * *

The lyrics sang out to the guests and the music serenaded the couple who were so in love. Lesley had died every day waiting for Marie. The song was their story.

As Lesley stepped towards her soon-to-be wife, every memory of binding her chest, every memory of hidden periods and haircuts she didn't want, fell from her. She wasn't afraid anymore.

Like a butterfly, Lesley emerged from her chrysalis as she stepped out of her old shell into herself. Marie came forward to take Lesley's hands tenderly in her own. Never, in her wildest dreams, could Lesley have wished for a more perfect day. Their two hearts stepped together.

Outside, spiralling like little wedding wishes finding their mark, the sparkling snowflakes continued to fall.

10. A GIFT FROM SANTA

Santa adjusted his belt and scratched his chin through his fluffy, white beard. Should he stop for a cup of tea or just carry on with this last job tonight? Although not discernible to the human eye, his eyes detected a very slight change in the light. Dawn was coming . . . No, he'd stop for a tea. Santa loved his job, but he'd learnt over the years that you couldn't run yourself ragged. It was a marathon not a sprint and he really did need a cup of tea.

Santa fished around in the footwell of the sleigh for his backpack. He pulled out his flask and picnic blanket and looked for a good place to sit on the roof. The reindeer shuffled to find a comfortable standing spot. They were used to the stop-start of the job. Their fur was sweaty under the harnesses. As they shuffled, a gentle, 'Jingle, jingle, jingle.' joined the winter night's breeze that was navigating its way around the sleeping city.

Santa enjoyed his tea. He found it quite refreshing. He found it gave him time to contemplate and double-check his thinking.

Santa had finished his present giving for the

night. That is to say, the physical presents. But there was another side to his job that the folklore missed. Like any story you focus on the obvious shining baubles and the detail tends to get omitted. The truth was that Santa's gift giving was a little more complex than folklore.

How many times, when money was tight, was there enough for Christmas? How was it, that despite the difficulties and struggles, so many families tried, for the sake of kindness, to make the best of any situation or feud at Christmas? How often was it that good, nice things seemed to happen around Christmas, or even just after?

Santa was able to grant these gifts because people asked for help and because they believed. Even when they didn't realise they had asked; all those silent prayers were heard by Santa. And this was his season. This was when his powers to grant wishes were at their greatest.

Santa replaced the lid on the flask and wiped the back of his glove over his mouth, catching the drips on his beard before they froze.

His eyes twinkled in the darkness and a warm, fuzzy feeling filled his tummy. He would particularly enjoy this one.

Replacing his flask and picnic blanket in the backpack, Santa walked over to the nearest boiler vent. It didn't need to be a physical chimney, it just needed to be a way in. He placed his finger on the side of his nose and just like a missing slide from a film reel; he was gone.

The bedroom smelt of spicy, earthy deodorant. Dirty clothes and used rugby kits were piled on the floor. Santa tried not to trip in the darkness. That wouldn't do at all!

Santa manoeuvred his sizeable tummy past the chest of drawers, where a small glass of milk and a cookie were balanced on the last uncluttered corner. Little tears pricked his eyes. Even after all these years he was humbled by human kindness, and the human propensity, despite all the odds, to hope and believe.

Santa looked over at Jonathan snoring loudly in his unwashed bedding. He knew, that despite the teasing, despite the incredulity of his peers, that he secretly wanted to believe. Jonathan just didn't talk about it. It had been nearly twenty years since he had last left a gift for Santa and asked for what he wanted for Christmas, but now that he'd asked, Santa was able to help.

Moving over to the guinea pig cage, Santa clicked open the door and peered inside. In the darkness Santa saw two, little, black, bead-like eyeballs blinking back at him. Placing his hand inside like a little step, the guinea pig hopped on. Santa gave the little fellow a reassuring stroke over his brown and white fur and placed him in his breast pocket, as he navigated his way back across the messy bedroom.

* * *

Cecilia woke to a beautiful, crisp, Christmas

morning. She pushed her red hair back from her face as she lay back on her pillow. She'd had an incredible dream.

Cecilia dreamt she'd heard beautiful, jingling bells. In her dream she was dancing around a giant Christmas tree, adorned with rainbow-coloured fairy lights. The melodic jingling made her feel warm and safe. She'd been talking to a lovely old man. She was telling him how lonely she was, how all her friends were married or engaged, or at least in love. How she felt unwanted and unlovable.

He'd listened attentively to her, and when she finished, he told her she was very much loved and that everyone had the right to be loved. That it wasn't easy, but to share your heart with another human was certainly a very worthwhile and rewarding wish.

It seemed so silly now, but in her dreams, having him reassure her and give her a big hug had made her feel so warm and happy. As if, waking up this morning, all her fears about being alone had melted away.

Cecilia laughed at herself in the cold, bright, light of morning. Very likely, the dream was nothing more than a result of leaving out milk and mince pie for Santa the night before. She wasn't sure what had made her do it. Daft, childish traditions. At least nobody would know.

Cecilia was unable to travel back home to family this year. This was her first Christmas alone in her flat. It was fine. She'd talk to friends and video call her family. There were lots of virtual catch ups that she'd have today. She planned to eat some yummy gourmet duck breast for her Christmas lunch and she had a whole bottle of prosecco to herself. She also had several Christmas romcoms that she'd saved for today. It would be fine.

With an eyebrow half-raised at herself for putting food out for Santa, Cecilia got out of bed to clear away the milk and mince pie that she'd left by the old fireplace in her bedroom.

'Oh no!' Cecilia exclaimed. The glass of milk had been knocked over onto her cream carpet and the mince pie looked as if it had been *eaten* by something.

'Rats!' she exclaimed in horror, guessing who the mystery muncher must be. Rushing out of the bedroom and slamming the door, Cecilia fished around in the kitchen for a rolling pin and plastic bowl. Her plan was to first catch the rat, then to do her best to save the carpet.

Cecilia gingerly re-entered the bedroom armed against the tiny intruder. Closing the door she tiptoed over to the bed, slowing lowering herself to floor level. She lifted the counterpane and shone the flashlight from her phone underneath the bed. Two, little, black eyes flashed back at her.

Cecilia jumped back in shock before she could really register what she saw. When her heart had stopped racing, she peaked back again. Little reflective eyes shone in the dark. A small, pudgy, brown-and-white face turned to her, and the creature said, ‘Squeak.’

‘Oh! Little sausage!’ exclaimed Cecilia, ‘How on earth did you get here?’

With a little persuasion and some lettuce, Cecilia managed to encourage the tiny, furry bundle out from under the bed and snugged up to her chest. She stroked it gently.

Furrowing her brow, she said out loud, ‘How on earth did you get in here little one?’

* * *

Jonathan woke with a bit of a hangover. Silly really. He'd been feeling lonely the night before, so he’d decided to drink whisky and look at pictures of his ex-girlfriends. Which had made him feel even worse, and to compensate he’d drunk even more.

He didn’t remember going to bed last night. Luckily, he didn’t have to go anywhere. He was in his flat alone this year. It was fine. It was just another day, right? Besides he had little Harry to keep him company.

Cutting up some carrot sticks Jonathan returned to the bedroom. The carrot sticks fell from his hands onto the pile of dirty clothes on his floor, as he opened his mouth in horror. Harry’s cage was open and Harry wasn’t inside.

‘It’s ok.’ he reasoned to himself, ‘He must be in the flat somewhere. As long as I’m not standing on him.’ Jonathan gingerly picked up each foot from the clothing pile underneath him and guiltily checked. He really needed to do something about living in such a mess. He could have squashed poor Harry without even realising.

Jonathan searched and searched. He whistled and called. He dangled food and swished flashlights under furniture, but he couldn't find Harry. He was gutted. The only thing he could find was a small glass of milk and a cookie he must have drunkenly left out for Santa the night before. So much for Christmas presents. His was missing.

Jonathan was really upset. He reasoned that he'd give the flat another search (to no avail) then get dressed and knock on the neighbour's doors, in case Harry had somehow got into the pipes or ventilation systems. The longer Harry was missing the more upset Jonathan felt. This was the worst Christmas ever.

* * *

A loud knock announced itself on Cecilia's door. It was just coming up to lunch and Cecilia had been discussing with Holly (the guinea pig) the complexities of her friend's relationship and why her friend's boyfriend was absolutely the wrong guy.

Cecilia jumped at the knock and Holly wrinkled her nose.

'It must be someone responding to the Facebook advert.' said Cecilia sadly. 'I'll be sorry to see you go little one.' Cecilia affectionately stroked Holly's little head and walked over to the front door. She peeped through the viewer. To her surprise there stood a six foot man in a rugby shirt. "Probably the kid's dad." she thought, before calling, 'Who is it?'

'Hi!' a deep voice resonated back. 'I've come about my guinea pig?' Cecilia raised an eyebrow. 'One of your neighbours said you'd posted an advert? Saying you'd found one? I think it might be mine.'

Cecilia hesitated for a second. If he was a burglar come to steal her five presents, then it was a good story. Could the guinea pig really be his? Seemed a little odd. 'Just a second.' she called in reply and pulled back the security chain.

Cecilia opened the door to Adonis in jogging bottoms. She could swear she could see his muscles under his rugby shirt. Her face started to flush slightly, matching her flame red hair.

'Sorry to bother you.' Jonathan explained. 'I've lost my guinea pig Harry, he's white and brown, he's a lovely fellow. One of your neighbours said you might have seen him or have him?' his eyes pleaded at her, he looked really upset and worried. As strange as it seemed Cecilia believed him.

'It's ok.' she said reassuringly, 'I have him in here, in the kitchen.'

'What!' said Jonathan in shock.

'I'm not cooking him!' Cecilia retorted back. The awkwardness broke and they both laughed. 'Come on in.' she said in a friendly manner, ushering him through the door.

Jonathan was impressed. The flat was as

beautiful as the occupant and just as immaculate. He felt scruffy and awkward, and he possibly smelt slightly of alcohol. Luckily whatever he smelt of seemed to be superseded by something delicious cooking in the kitchen – and not Harry luckily.

Jonathan followed Cecilia through to the kitchen and there was little Harry, in a cardboard box, lined with a towel and munching on some carrot sticks.

'Oh Harry!' Jonathan exclaimed and rushed over to the box. He held his little pet aloft and kissed him gently on the head. 'I'm mighty happy to see you buddy.'

Cecilia felt her heart melt. What a lovely guy. She couldn't help herself as the words tumbled out, 'Why don't you both stay for lunch, that is, if you've nothing else to do?' she suddenly felt very stupid, he probably had a girlfriend, her cheeks flamed.

Jonathan had never in his life felt that he'd wanted to be somewhere, as much as he wanted to be here. It felt like home, she felt like home. It was as if he'd been searching for this place his whole life and actually it was little Harry that had found it for him. He looked into her beautiful, hazel eyes and said, 'That would be great. You don't mind? I'm not disturbing you?'

Cecilia's heart soared as she said, 'Not at all. It's just me. I'm cooking duck, I know it's not traditional. Is that ok?'

'I love duck!'

Cecilia sized up Jonathan. Luckily, she always cooked more than she needed to have an easy meal ready for tomorrow, but she thought that some last-minute "pigs in blankets" wouldn't hurt – even though it was an unusual side to duck. The Christmas pudding should be enough for them both. Yes, she could do it.

Cecilia smiled back at him. 'So do I.' she said. Then she conversationally added, 'Merry Christmas . . .' she paused.

'Oh, it's Jonathan, my name's Jonathan.' he came towards her to shake her hand. Electricity ran through them as they touched. 'And you are? Cecilia? I think your neighbour said?'

'Yes,' she replied, smiling up at him, 'Cecilia.' They beamed at each other and time stopped for a moment. 'I don't suppose you are any good at opening up prosecco?' Cecilia enquired.

'On it!' Jonathan replied. Giving little Harry an affectionate scratch on his head before putting him back in the cardboard box, Jonathan headed to the fridge.

As easily as that, Cecilia and Jonathan opened their Christmas presents from Santa. And if you listened carefully, somewhere on the breeze, you could just about hear, a very quiet, very happy, 'Ho, ho, ho!' and a barely discernible jingle of little, tiny bells.

11. ALL I WANT FOR CHRISTMAS

And that was it. That's how it finished. A beautiful love story, a heart-melting romance. Ended with a hug, and an 'I'm sorry.' and an 'It's ok, it just didn't work out.'

As Ellie left their flat, she wondered if she would ever see him again. She knew in her heart she would never stop loving him. But he wasn't willing to love her back and she needed that.

Ellie was brought back to now. The kettle clicked as it rolled to a boil. She was glad to make herself cup of tea. She needed the warmth today. She pushed back her fluffy blonde hair with her tanned, toned fingers, and reached up to the cupboard for a mug.

Ellie looked around her beautiful kitchen. Just her style. White, shaker-style cabinets and marble counter tops. On the kitchen island sat her discarded, half-read magazine; some fruit; her phone; some small, jelly-like dinosaurs the kids had hatched from a gooey, dinosaur egg; and a legal letter.

She poured the hot water into the mug and let the

tea stew. The problem, she reflected, was her. None of her relationships worked out. Perhaps she asked too much. She really needed to go to counselling and work this all out. That was why she originally left *him* all those years ago and why she was divorcing now. Neither of them were willing to work on a relationship. It wasn't always easy and she got that, but she wanted to work on it. And if she was the only person willing to work on the relationship then that meant she was the only one invested and "in" right?

Ellie knitted her brows together as she poured in the milk. The problem with Scott (her current ex-husband) was that she had never loved him like *that.* She knew what real, heart-stopping love looked and felt like; the way everything you said or did together was special, everything you touched was magical and meaningful, the way that you couldn't imagine a future without the other person. The way you could never walk away. But she did. Twice.

Scott had ticked all the boxes; he was the right fit, he wanted all the right things, she felt like she should have been in love, she convinced herself that she had been in love. But the love had felt different than before. Scott had wanted to marry. Ellie had wanted kids. When she'd found out about Scott's other life: his multiple affairs, she wasn't really that bothered. It hurt her pride but she was able to walk away and close the door. She had no problem being civil for the sake of the children because she wasn't emotionally invested. At all.

Ellie looked again at the legal letter on the countertop. Her divorce was finalised. She was single again. She was free. But her thoughts always returned to her first love and the way that had felt. It was as fresh in her heart as if it was yesterday. She could still feel what it was like to love.

* * *

Ellie's sons, Benjamin and Robert, were super excited to go to the Christmas market fair after school on Friday. The council had blocked off one of the main streets in the town. It was filled the with Christmas market stalls and rides, including a large Ferris wheel.

Ellie was excited too. It was early December and she could do with some new decorations, to get herself in the mood to start decorating the house for Christmas.

They bundled themselves up with scarves and gloves against the cold December evening and piled into the car. Ben and Robbie were as high as kites, which inevitably meant some squabbling. Ellie was quite relieved to get into town and park up, so she could get them out of the car and into the fresh air.

The Christmas market was ablaze with lights, noise and colour. It was also very busy. The street had been closed off either side and there was a queue for ten minutes to get in, however, it was worth it. The Christmas market made everyone feel festive and Ellie was happy to give the boys their freedom while she looked at the stalls. She gave them some money and they arranged to meet back in an hour for some food.

The crafts on the market stalls were exquisite. Ellie gravitated towards the first stall on the street. It was adorned with white fairly lights, over the awning and inside the stall. The table displayed little candle lamps with Christmas scenes etched onto the shades. One had some deer standing in a pine forest; another was of falling snowflakes, each one was a different shape; yet another had a lovely nativity scene. Ellie liked the nativity scene the best. Putting her purchase safety in her bag she moved to the next stall, which had hand-carved tree decorations.

Ellie let her mind wander . . . As it happened, she hadn't seen *him* again. She thought she would, after all those years of being together, she thought they would stay friends. He met a teacher shortly afterwards and they quickly fell pregnant. Suddenly Ellie had become the other woman. The teacher had refused to meet her. She texted congratulations on their daughter's birth, but her message was blocked. She was blocked. Perhaps that had soured her last relationship with Scott? Perhaps she had pushed Scott into the arms of other women.

Shaking her head and shrugging her shoulders, Ellie reasoned that she would never know. She would never know why Scott had had affairs and why *he*, Dave, hadn't loved her.

'Dave!' The shock was unreal. It was as if he was a hallucination standing in front of her. Except the hallucination had aged. His black hair was flecked with grey, even so he still looked slightly like a "Ken doll". It had been, what, fifteen years since she had seen him? They had both aged. Forgetting the blocked texts and cut connections Ellie instantly smiled and touched his arm. 'Dave, it's me. It's Ellie.'

* * *

The reunion, after all these years, hadn't gone at all how she expected.

Dave had turned to her smiling, then recognising her, his smile dropped. He mechanically said, "Hello." They passed a few pleasantries. Ellie said she was divorced with two boys. Dave said he'd recently moved back to the area, that he had a daughter, then that he had to go and look for her. And left.

Ellie was heartbroken. Of course she still loved him. Even after all these years. But it was because she loved him that (she consoled herself) she was glad he was happily married with a daughter. Her subconscious joked to her; at least he had a child to pass his good-looking genes onto!

Ellie talked over her hurt with her best friend from work later that week.

Jane said, 'You've seen him. He's happily married with his, I guess now teenage, daughter. Leave it.'

'I know. I guess I'm still broken-hearted that it didn't work out. I will always love him. Genuinely I'm happy for him.' Ellie poured her heart out to her friend with honesty. 'I look at my relationships and they're a mess. The only common denominator is me.'

'I wouldn't be so hard on yourself Els. You self-reflect. Most people don't. You have a big heart and you are genuinely happy for others. You don't resent their happiness.' Her friend Jane continued, 'Why did you leave him in the first place?'

'Oh.' Ellie let out a big sigh. Her friend had touched a sore spot. 'Many reasons. His mum tried to control the relationship and he let her; he couldn't stand up for me; but really, the real reason was, he wouldn't kiss me. I had to ask for physical affection, I knew it wasn't right. I tried to do counselling but he refused, so eventually I gave up. I couldn't face reaching sixty years old and not being kissed.'

Jane tried to lighten the atmosphere. 'Well, if he's had a daughter, he's obviously kissed somebody!'

Ellie was glad of her friend's wit and they both laughed.

* * *

'Well,' Ellie reasoned out loud, as she finished the last of the decorations in the house and looked around appreciatively at the result, 'you may be single, but you can certainly enjoy the little things.' Ellie liked doing, the things she liked doing, such as: decorating the house, her job, her children, having her hair done, her hobbies of painting and reading. Ellie enjoyed her life. She didn't need a man to fulfil her.

It was funny to think that the reason she'd left Dave all those years ago was because she couldn't face reaching sixty without being kissed, yet here she was, divorced and single, and not desperate to quickly partner into another doomed relationship. Perhaps, after all, she wouldn't be kissing anyone when she was sixty. Ironic really.

Ellie wrapped the last of the boy's presents ready to put them under the tree. She had the day off work to do all the bits she couldn't do when she was around them. It was only when she was wrapping, she realised there were a few things she'd forgotten. No bother. She'd pop into town after lunch.

The town was buzzing with the Christmas season. As it was a weekday it was a little quieter than the weekends, but it was still busy.

Christmas was one of Ellie's favourite seasons. She loved how everyone was kind and happy. She loved the lights and decorations. She loved the carols. She was perfectly happy to collect the last few presents and be in the Christmassy buzz.

Ellie decided to stop at a coffee shop before heading home. It was cosy and artisan, with large wooden tables and benches for several people to sit and converse. The cakes were homemade; they had special, spicy teas; Christmas enhanced coffees; and seasonal hot chocolate, which involved extra cream, marshmallows and sparkly chocolate sprinkles.

Ellie happily dug her fork into a large piece of chocolate cake as she watched the cream start to sink into her hot chocolate. She was grateful for her life. She was lucky.

'Hello again.' a man's voice said. Ellie looked up, to see Dave. She nearly choked on her cake. She thought she'd put that ghost, in her heart, to rest. Inelegantly wiping her face with a napkin, she stood up.

'Oh hi! Hi. How are you?' she said.

Dave smiled in his soft, kind way. 'Yes great. Thank you. I've popped out from work to get some last-minute presents.'

'Yes, me too.' Ellie motioned to her bags under the bench and smiled. 'Are you getting a drink?'

'Yes, I thought I'd stop for a coffee.'

'You are more than welcome to join me, if you like.' As soon as she said it, she regretted it. She watched him hesitate. She felt like the crazy, stalker, ex-girlfriend.

'Yes.' he replied. 'That would be nice, I'll be back in a minute.'

Ellie's mind was blank as she waited for Dave to pay and join her. She knew intimately every one of his mannerisms. The way he interacted with people. The cake and coffee he would choose. It was like a reunion with a long-lost family member. It felt odd.

They chatted comfortably for half an hour. Dave had updated her on his job moves and the family. His brother had divorced and was living back with his parents. His daughter had just started at the local secondary school, and that he too had divorced, just recently.

Ellie tried to gloss over it. It was strange finding out these details from his life. She didn't want to pry. She tried to keep things light. But as easy as that, in this café, there they were, just the two of them in a crazy world, two souls reconnecting.

All too quickly, it ended. They exchanged phone numbers and addresses and agreed they would meet up again soon. Then they separated, on their way back to their busy different lives.

As Ellie carried the shopping back to the car she thought, "Well at least I got to see him one last time. I'm glad he is happy."

* * *

It was Christmas Eve. Scott wasn't interested in having the boys over for Christmas. He'd left some presents for them, and then he was off, in his big, posh, expensive, white four-by-four. The boys were a little hurt, but they played computer games and tried not to show it.

When Ellie came into Ben's bedroom with some

snacks and drinks, she managed to prod a little into their feelings.

'You're not too upset you're not with your dad for Christmas?' she asked.

'No.' said Robbie.

'Ben? How do you feel about it?' Ellie enquired.

'Well, to be honest mum, I think he's forgotten about us now, and I'd rather be home with you anyway.'

'Oh boys, of course he hasn't forgotten about you. I know he loves you very much.'

'I don't think you're right mum.' Robbie replied. 'He's more interested in the new baby.'

Ellie was silent. Oh. She didn't know about that. Well, none of her business she supposed. Not now.

'Even if you are to get another little sister or brother, I know your dad will always love you.' she said.

Silence. She'd pushed the probing far enough. She left the bedroom to go and watch a house renovation programme on catch-up and maybe eat a mince pie.

As she pinged the mince pie warm in the microwave the doorbell rang. They weren't expecting anyone. She peered through the safety viewer in the door. It was Dave.

Quickly she checked her appearance in the hall mirror. She looked all right. A little older, a little wrinkled, nothing special, normal. Ellie opened the door.

'Hi . . .' she stopped mid-greeting. Dave was

sobbing. Her heart skipped a beat. Her eyes welled up with sympathy. 'Goodness. Come in.' she said.

Ellie ushered Dave through to the kitchen. Once she had settled him down at the kitchen island and offered tissues, she asked, 'Tea?'

Dave nodded weepily, his red eyes looking back at her gratefully. The boys were upstairs playing their games. The kitchen was quiet except for the occasional sniffle from Dave. Ellie passed Dave his tea and in doing so rubbed him on the shoulders.

'You ok?' she asked gently.

He nodded slowly, while she sat down next to him. Obviously he wasn't. He dabbed the tissue to his eyes and nose, then asked, 'Why did you leave me?'

Ellie was stunned. Out of all the things she expected to hear, it wasn't that. She replied slowly, 'Well . . . you wouldn't stand up for me, you wouldn't go to counselling and you wouldn't kiss me.'

'I wouldn't kiss you because you were too perfect. I wouldn't go to counselling because I was afraid you would leave. I could see the discord growing between you and my mother and I was helpless to stop it. I didn't know what to do. Then you did leave. And my life has only ever been in half-light since. I've tried to find happiness. I loved my wife and I love my daughter. But now they are together at Christmas and I'm all alone. Again.' He sobbed hard into the tissue.

Ellie felt awful. She felt like some thoughtless,

feelingless bully. Willing to trample over those she loved if she didn't get her way.

Behind Dave, in the doorway to the kitchen stood Robbie. Ellie shook her head "no" and put her finger to her lips. He looked puzzled and wandered back upstairs.

Ellie shuffled her stool a little nearer and put her arm around Dave's shoulders. 'Hey, hey, shhh, don't get upset about it, hey, shhh, shhh.' The truth was, she was crying too. 'I left because you didn't seem to want to be with me and you weren't willing to work on it. I had to ask for affection. I just felt like something was wrong. You didn't ask me to stay.'

Dave sobbed harder. This wasn't helping. She rubbed his back and tried to calm him, saying, 'Hey, hey, hey. Shhh.'

Finally, he asked, 'And now? Are you willing to work on it now if I was to ask you to stay?'

Ellie gulped. Could she risk her heart again? What if it was the same?

Dave continued, 'Or is it really you that's not willing to work on it?' The comment stung.

Ellie scrambled to reply, 'I understand. I have always loved you and I always will. But so much has happened. We have children. We've both been divorced.'

'I think you're the one that's scared.'

'I can't just go back to the way things were.' she replied. He looked at her with disbelief.

Ellie's walls of justification came tumbling down

as she realised, she was the problem. She was the problem in all her relationships, and that true love, real love, was rare. Suddenly she decided to be brave, she had no time to think, her time was now.

Ellie replied, 'I can't guarantee the future, I don't know what will happen. But if we were to take things slowly. If we were able to get a professional counsellor to help guide us through the mess of our history and give us the tools to deal with our future –' Ellie gulped. She was scared. This was going to be hard. 'Yes. I'll give it a try.'

They clasped each other tightly. His embrace was warm, his scent was familiar. She felt like she was coming home.

When they finally parted, he stoked her cheek and said, 'I didn't think I'd ever see you again.'

His touch was as familiar as her own hand. She reached up and held his hand in hers.

After a few moments she suggested, 'Well, how about a first date with my boys? Would you like to join us for Christmas lunch tomorrow?'

Dave blinked back the tears and nodded. They embraced again. And that is just how Ben and Robbie found them nearly an hour later.

12. CHRISTMAS TREE

Sylvia stood by the satsumas. The gorgeous Christmas scent filled her nose and took her back . . . She was six years old, sitting on her dad's knee. It was Christmas morning. Her younger brother was playing with his farm set (that their dad had built the week before). Cows and pigs lay scattered over the living room floor. Her brother was moving a tractor in and out of the fields and making tractor noises, '*Brrr. Brrr. Brrr. Chug. Chug.*'

Sylvia's dad, as always, was wearing his cap to keep out the draught. He had his arms gently around her, holding her safe, while she arranged the dress on her new doll. The dress was made of layers of pink tulle and covered in little stars. I was her favourite present so far.

Sylvia and her brother had just opened their stockings, which were jam-packed with goodies. And at the bottom there was always an apple and a satsuma . . .

Sylvia re-lived those happily memories as clearly as if they were yesterday. She had many happy childhood memories, but her happiest were Christmas memories. Christmas was her favourite time of year.

As Sylvia stood by the satsumas in the supermarket, she soaked it all in: the smell, the happy shoppers – as everyone seemed a little kinder at this time of year, the sparkly decorations which hung between the aisles, and the Christmas carols playing in the background. She could feel the anticipation building and she was starting to feel very festive!

Sylvia loved the month of December. She spent the time on her crafts and her Christmas preparations: handmaking cards, painting pinecones and baking batches of mince pies. This year she was going to make some mince pies for the family next door, as she loved doing things for others. Sylvia also needed to order her tree. Sniffing the air she could almost smell it now. A very happy memory flooded back to her . . .

* * *

'Hayside Garden Centre. How can we help you?' said a man's voice.

'Oh hello. I'd like to place an order for my Christmas tree please. I'd like it delivered on the nineteenth of December if that's possible?'

'Yes madam, we have delivery dates available then. What variety of tree are you looking for? We have Nordmann Fir, Norway Spruce and Fraser Fir.'

'Norway Spruce please, I always have a Norway Spruce.' Sylvia could smell it already.

* * *

Sylvia knocked on the bright-red door and turned to watch the snow falling lightly on an assortment of toys that had been enjoyed and abandoned in the garden. She smiled remembering when her children were little. It seemed like yesterday. In reality they were grown up and planning their own families now.

'Oh Mrs Richardson!' Louise said, as she opened the door to her generous neighbour.

Sylvia held up the still warm mince pies in the tin. 'Something for everyone to enjoy!' she said.

'We were just about to have a cup of tea. These will be perfect.' Louise turned behind her to the chaotic hallway and shouted, 'Olivia! Theo! Mrs Richardson has a treat for you.'

Sylvia loved the sound of scampering across the ceiling and hearing the herd of elephants coming down the stairs. She shivered slightly in the doorway.

'Goodness, do, do come in.' said Louise. Ushering Sylvia through into the hall.

Closing the door, Louise took Sylvia on through to the yellow and cream kitchen, with a beautiful Aga, pine table and matching chairs. All sorts were strewn across the table: some children's Christmas puzzles, a few women's magazines, a screwdriver set, a fruit bowl and a small, red poinsettia.

Louise hastily stacked some of the items and

made room for Sylvia. The children sat down around her and started to demolish the mince pies. You might think that Louise would restrain them, but she looked on, smiling, as they ate at least four each. Well, thought Sylvia, at least her efforts were appreciated and everyone was happy.

'Tea Mrs Richardson?' Louise looked at her neighbour sympathetically.

'Oh, that would be lovely, thank you.'

The cheer of the Christmas season surrounded them all like a warm hug that Sylvia so desperately needed this year.

* * *

The decorating of the Christmas tree had always been done by Sylvia's mother. Her mum had come from a very artistic family and their tree always looked beautiful: delicate, glass baubles (that they weren't allowed to touch!); multi-coloured, petal-like, fairy lights with glitter delicately clinging to the edges; slim, expensive, elegant tinsel, draped expertly from branch to branch; and little, glass "icicles" that fell from the branches and glinted in the rainbow-colours of the fairy lights. When the living room lights were out, and only a few table lamps on, then the tree was at its most beautiful, and to a young Sylvia it almost seemed magical. The smell of pine made it seem as if they were in a forest. Everything about Charismas enchanted Sylvia.

Sylvia looked expectantly out of the window and checked her watch again. Three-thirty. The tree should have been delivered by now. Sylvia felt a little agitated and tried to take her mind off it. She turned on the radio to listen to *Carols from Kings*.

By five-thirty the tree still hadn't arrived. She rang the garden centre with a slight hint of irritation in her voice.

'I'm so sorry Mrs Richardson, but we don't have any record of you ordering a tree.' a man said.

Sylvia asserted, 'I ordered it three weeks ago.'

'I'm sorry, unfortunately we are out of Norway Spruce, but we do have some sizes left in the Nordmann Fir?'

Sylvia sighed. It just wasn't the same. 'No thank you. I'll try somewhere else.' she said.

Sylvia was upset and annoyed. She thought of the dusty, fake tree in the attic. But she hated fake trees and for the moment her heart wasn't in it. Disappointment sat in her chest like a large lump of undigested Christmas pudding.

Sylvia tried to distract herself. She went out to the back garden to put some more food on the bird table. A cheery voice shouted over the fence, 'Hello! Mrs Richardson!' It was Louise from next door. Sylvia gave a half-smile and wandered over to the fence.

Louise noticed Sylvia didn't seem herself and asked what was wrong. Louise listened carefully and at the end of the story said, 'Well I have a good idea. Instead of you going up into that dusty attic, why don't I send Mike up? He can get the tree down for you and set it up. Also, we have some spare outdoor lights that we aren't going to use. We'd be delighted if you'd let us put them up for you this year? Especially after everything you have done for us.' Louise thought to herself, "And everything you have been through this year."

Sylvia felt her spirits lift a little, as she bravely thought, "This is what Christmas is about: people doing nice things for each other." Graciously she accepted the offer.

Louise continued, 'The children and I are going to start wrapping presents. We also have roast beef planned for dinner. Why don't you come and join us?' Sylvia hadn't even thought about dinner. Roast beef with them all sounded lovely, she'd also be glad of the company right now.

'I'd love to.' Sylvia said.

'Come round in half an hour.' Louise instructed.

* * *

Sylvia knocked on the front door and Mike answered. 'Do come in Mrs Richardson.' he said, as he ushered her into the hall. The hall was still its usual state of chaos, with the addition of Mike's toolbox. Sylvia handed him her house keys and explained how to get into the attic.

Mike put a reassuring hand on her shoulder and said, 'Don't worry. I will have it looking lovely for you.' There was a twinkle in his eye.

The children came bursting through to the hall and dragged Sylvia off to the kitchen, where wrapping paper and accessories seemed to cover everything. Someone had also been a little liberal with the glitter, and most items, including the children, appeared to be twinkling. Sylvia decided she was all-in.

When dinner was ready, they all worked to clear the kitchen table, but Mike still wasn't back.

'I'll give him a phone.' said Louise. Picking up her mobile she called him. 'How's it going? . . . Uh-huh . . . Uh-huh . . . Good . . . Great . . . All done? Right, that's fine . . . We're ready to serve up now . . . Just wash your hands . . .That's fine, no one will mind the cobwebs.' Turning back to the room Louise said, 'He's on his way back.'

They had a lovely dinner together. Lots of joking and laughing; Sylvia felt her heart warm, she felt good. The beef was excellent and was accompanied by yorkshire puddings and mustard. Sylvia thought she wouldn't manage the apple pie and cream for dessert, but somehow, she did, even though her tummy was bursting.

When dinner was over and Sylvia went to the hall to put on her coat and go home, she found the whole family followed her. She looked round in surprise.

'Well. Night-night.' Sylvia said, kissing the children on their cheeks. 'Thank you again for a lovely meal.'

'But aren't we going to come?' said Theo. Louise

gave his arm a shove and he placed his hand over his mouth.

Mike took up on the theme. 'Good idea young Theo. It's pretty late and you never know who's about.'

So Sylvia left her neighbours house, followed by her neighbours. When she got outside, she saw that Mike had done a wonderful job with the outdoor lights. Little icicles framed all the way along her roof, and her open porch had an extra set of lights to welcome visitors.

'Oh, they're lovely.' Sylvia said, squeezing Louise's hand and beaming up at Mike, in the glow of the twinkling lights.

'But what about . . .' Theo started, before his mum clamped her hand over his mouth.

Louise smiled sheepishly as she said, 'Let's walk Mrs Richardson to her front door.'

Sylvia had the distinct feeling something was going on but didn't know how to argue with her kind neighbours, so all five of them walked up the garden path and the family watched as she put her key in the lock.

'Well, goodnight again.' she said politely. The family watched her walk in the door. Wave. And close the door.

Putting on the hall light Sylvia couldn't help but think it was all a little odd.

Hanging up her coat Sylvia wandered through to the living room, but before she could turn on the light, the multi-coloured Christmas tree lights sparkled their magic on her. She stood there speechless and in awe. She hadn't seen it before because Mike had thoughtfully closed the curtains.

In front of her a magnificent Norway Spruce proudly stood, decorated in multi-coloured lights, baubles and hung with glass icicles – just like the Christmas trees from when she was a child. Sylvia burst into tears as the smell of the Norway Spruce filled her nose . . . suddenly she was standing in front of a Christmas tree, eighteen years old, with her boyfriend Geoff, he was holding a ring . . .

Sylvia came back to now and touched the worn band of the diamond solitaire ring on her left hand. This was her first Christmas without him. Standing in the multi-coloured, fairy light glow it almost felt magical, as if Geoff was standing with her right now, wishing her "Happy Christmas." or proposing to her all over again. Sylvia rushed back to the front door and opened it to a laughing, expectant family.

'Happy Christmas!' they cheered.

'But how?' Sylvia stumbled over her words, tears streaming down her cheeks.

Louise stepped forward to hug her. 'I'm so sorry,' she said. 'We didn't mean to upset you.'

'No, not at all, it's a wonderful Christmas surprise.' Sylvia sobbed.

Louise stood with her arm around Sylvia and explained, 'I don't really like real trees you see. It's the mess. But Mike wanted one this year, so we bought one and had it in the garage. Hearing your story today, we thought that you would appreciate the tree more than us, especially this year, and that it would make the most wonderful "Thank you." for all the kind things you do for us.' Louise winked. 'And I won't have so much cleaning up to do after Christmas!' Louise tried to lighten the atmosphere and distract the old lady from crying. She said teasingly, 'Mike has quite a flair for decorating, don't you think?' Sylvia wholeheartedly agreed and hugged them all.

Everyone was a little late to bed that night. But Sylvia remembered that first Christmas without Geoff as the smell of mince pies, while singing carols badly, grouped round a real Norway Spruce Christmas tree.

13. TURKEY FOR LUNCH

Maria felt hot and flustered. It was the same every Christmas morning. She was in the kitchen, alone, getting lunch ready, checking the timings, remembering what needed to come out of the fridge or oven when. No matter how many years she did this, she always found it stressful. Because it was Christmas and because the family would be expecting a wonderful lunch.

Maria was stressed for other reasons too. Their daughter Frances was back from her first term at university, during which time Maria and Paul had spent many late nights talking to Frances on the phone. Frances didn't seem to be having a good time at all. She thought she was going to fail the first set of January exams and the course. She didn't have a solid friendship group. She felt awkward and out of place. Maria so desperately wanted her to be happy. She just wished she could be there to hold her hand, just as when Frances was four years old, secure in her grasp, looking up to Maria for smiles and sunshine.

Their son Jason, who finished university in the summer, ended his education with a degree and a boyfriend. It had been a shock initially, but not because they were against it. More that it was so unexpected. And this was the Christmas they were due to meet Charlie, as Jason had invited his boyfriend for Christmas lunch. To be honest Maria was worried that Charlie would find them outdated and old fashioned, that he might be offended by something they accidentally said. What worried Maria most was that she would say something that would hurt Charlie's feelings. The thought turned her tummy into knots.

Jason, Maria's only son, was her absolute world. He'd always been a tender, sensitive boy. If she could have bubble wrapped him and put him in a golden cage she would have gladly done so. But she knew that he had to go out into the world, to be his own man, to mark his own density. She just hadn't anticipated that he was gay. Maria desperately wanted Jason to be ok and happy. And she certainly didn't want to be the reason his heart got broken. Nothing in the world would be more abhorrent than alienating Charlie and therefore hurting Jason. Maria shuddered at the thought of it as if someone had walked over her grave.

Carefully Maria rewrapped some of the pigs in blankets. Smoothing her apron, she looked around the hot kitchen for the next job to do. Jason and Charlie would be here in an hour. The turkey needed to come out in thirty minutes, then the potatoes could go back in on high heat, on the top shelf to crisp.

There was another reason Maria was worried, but this was so subtle, so unseen, that Maria herself was hardly aware of why this concerned her so much.

Maria and Paul had always been close: lovers, friends and partners. They were like vines that had intertwined and grown into one. And then. Then silence. They rarely talked. With Frances now at university the evenings were spent in front of the telly. Paul watched his sport and she read romantic novels on her Kindle. But she was desperately lonely. All she wanted was for Paul to kiss her again with love and passion, like he used to. The most she got was a polite peck on the cheek. The hurt gnawed away at her and it all seemed to be coming to a head. Today. At Christmas lunch.

Paul was in the living room. Doing something with the tree he said. Frances was in her bedroom studying. Maria opened the hot oven door and took out the turkey. Carefully she placed it under some foil to rest. The doorbell rang. Whipping off her apron she rushed into the hall. Frances wandered to the top of the stairs still in her pyjamas.

'Darling! You're not dressed!' Maria said in an exasperated tone.

'I didn't realise the time.' Frances replied. She held a well-used, empty, coffee mug in her hand. 'It's fine. No point putting on an act. Best Charlie sees how things are.'

Maria didn't want to argue and spoil the day.

But really! She so wanted today to be perfect. She wanted everything to be ok for Jason and for them to show their best side to Charlie.

Maria flapped her hands in the air and let out a deep sigh. She peeked her head round the living room door. Paul had his head in the Christmas tree doing *something.* Internally she despaired. Did she have to direct everyone to act reasonably?

'Paul.' Maria hissed. He jumped guiltily. 'Jason and Charlie are at the front door. Come on.' She motioned to him to come. Paul straightened his Christmas jumper and dutifully followed her to the front door.

Enthusiastically they opened the door to two winter wrapped young men and a huge dog.

'Mum! Dad!' Jason cried out cheerfully. 'Meet Charlie!' He turned to his boyfriend, who looked petrified beneath his perfectly handsome complexion. Charlie's dog, a Vizsla, bounded straight into the hall.

'Oh!' said Maria, beaming and looking extremely happy to have a huge dog in her hall. She turned back to the young men and tenderly hugged them both, with tears in her eyes. She didn't know why she felt so emotional. Standing back and admiring them she saw that they looked right together. Jason looked *happy.* A little fear that had holed up in her heart started to melt away.

Paul hugged his son and Charlie, enthusiastically slapping them on the back and ushering them in. Charlie's dog had already started sniffing the air in

Christmas anticipation.

'I hope you don't mind the dog Mum.' Jason said, a little too late. 'The dog minder we were going to leave him with let us down last-minute, so we had to bring him.' Jason's sensitive eyes connected with hers.

'Of course it is ok love.' Maria replied. To be honest she'd walk on nails to make Jason happy. She could cope with a dog!

'Well,' said Paul addressing Jason and Charlie, 'why don't you both chuck your coats on the stand, the presents under the tree and come with me for a predinner Christmas drink?'

Maria thought to herself, "I'd love to stop for a predinner Christmas drink too."

Almost as if Paul had read her mind, he said, 'You too love, I know you are busy, but perhaps just five minutes before you go back to the kitchen?'

'I have to do the potatoes and sausages.' Maria protested.

'I can do it Mum.' Frances piped up. She waved her dirty coffee cup in the air. 'Besides I need some more coffee.'

Maria was persuaded. 'Ok! Frances, the potatoes need to go on the top shelf, the pigs in blankets on the bottom shelf.'

Frances wandered off to the kitchen, as Maria, Paul, Charlie and Jason went into the living room for a drink. Maria actually felt herself relax a little bit.

Charlie was a little shorter than Maria had

expected, he was also quite skinny, but in a male model sort of way. He had dark-blonde hair that he'd grown long on the top and styled in a wave. His eyes were a beautiful deep-brown, and just as alert as Jason's. Maria had read about highly sensitive people, the sort of people that can read a room by just *knowing*, and she suspected that both Charlie and Jason were both such types of people. Almost as if their antennae had been turned up too high. They both seemed very alike and the perfect complement to each other. They clearly understood each other and almost seemed to communicate on a different wavelength to Maria. She didn't mind, so long as Jason was happy.

Frances popped her head around the door to update Maria on the cooking, then excused herself to get dressed. Frances exchanged a knowing look with her dad before heading upstairs.

Maria finished her sherry and also excused herself to finish the last of the preparations for lunch. Charlie and Jason insisted on laying the table, which was one less job for Maria to do, and Paul wanted to finish "fixing" the lights. Not that Maria could see much wrong with them. Best not to ask.

In her head Maria ran through the list of things still to do, as she walked from the living room to the kitchen. "Just the gravy to make and decanting the vegetables into serving dishes." Maria thought as she rushed along.

'Ahh!' Maria let out a huge, blood-curdling

scream.

The whole house stopped and held its breath.

There, in the middle of the kitchen, stood a large, rust-brown Vizsla with a turkey in its mouth.

Maria thought she was going to faint. Jason and Charlie rushed in. Charlie started apologising profusely. Paul put a reassuring arm around her. Maria desperately tried to tell Charlie and anyone else that would believe her, that, "It was ok, everything was fine." but the words just wouldn't come out. She thought for a minute she might be about to cry.

Paul started to manoeuvre her towards the living room, while Jason and Charlie wrestled with the turkey and the dog. She could hear Charlie scolding him as she stumbled into the living room, 'Naughty Louis, how could you? Bad dog. Very bad dog.'

After poor Louis had been confined to the back bathroom with a blanket and some water, Jason and Charlie came through to the living room with Frances, who had finally got dressed and was looking lovely in a Christmassy dress.

Maria just sat on the sofa in shock.

Jason knelt down in front of her and took her hands, 'Mum, don't you worry about a thing. We're going to sort it all. You just stay here with Charlie and we are going to finish Christmas lunch. It won't be what you planned but I promise you,' her darling little boy looked into her eyes, 'that we will have a lovely lunch. Ok?' She tried to smile and nod. He got up and kissed her on the forehead.

Poor Charlie! He carefully sat down next to Maria on the sofa and gave it his best shot to start a conversation with her.

* * *

With the demise of the turkey came something completely unexpected. A can-do willingness to get along and make the best of it. Calm and cooperation settled over the house like magical fairy dust.

A little while later Frances returned to the living room to find Charlie and her mum poring over old photo albums, eating chocolates and sipping sherry together. They were having a wonderful time as Maria recounted stories of Jason and Frances growing up.

'Lunch is served!' Frances announced proudly. Maria entered the dining room with trepidation – but she needn't have worried.

Little fairy lights adorned the mantlepiece and twinkled over the table. Some old candelabra had been brought out and little baubles dangled off the arms, catching the light and sending out little beams of colour, which hit the walls and the tablecloth. The old, pink-glass sundae bowls, which Jason and Frances used as children, had been rescued from the back of the sideboard, and a nostalgic prawn cocktail starter awaited them for their first course.

Maria felt herself relax. Charlie insisted on sitting next to her, which pleased her greatly. Louis was allowed out of his sin bin and had tried to unobtrusively place himself under the table. Jason and Frances were playing tricks on each other and telling their silly in-jokes, just as they'd done as teenagers. And Paul was wonderful. He was a rock. Organising it all. Sorting it all out. He opened the champagne and passed Maria the first glass.

Maria looked around and saw that everyone was *happy.* As they pulled crackers and put on flimsy, coloured-paper crowns, she tried not to think about what she was going to get for lunch. Instead, she made the best of her prawn cocktail and with everyone else laughed at the terrible cracker jokes.

Paul orchestrated Jason and Frances into action, to clear the sundae bowls and help him in the kitchen to bring in the main course.

It wasn't turkey. But that was ok. Paul had found the rump steaks Maria had been planning to cook tomorrow for dinner. To accompany their steak, they had delicious turkey gravy and pigs in blankets, with the roast potatoes, stuffing and vegetables Maria had already prepared. It was delicious!

Paul opened up a lovely bottle of red he'd been saving. It just seemed like the right time. And Charlie gave Maria a wink when he caught her sneaking a little sausage to Louis under the table.

By the time it came to the flaming Christmas pudding, the laughter had turned to cheering.

Frances had found some Christmas music on her phone and brought down her speakers from upstairs. After Paul's red wine, nearly everyone was convinced they either could sing or that they definitely knew all the words.

Quite simply it had turned into the best Christmas lunch Maria could remember. She caught Paul's eye. He winked at her. He could see she was happy.

Paul reached out his hand to touch hers and said, 'Maria darling, when we go through to the living room could you help me fix the Christmas tree lights?'

It wasn't at all what Maria had expected Paul to say. For a second, she thought he was joking. But he wasn't. She reasoned that, "That's what their relationship was now" and that "It couldn't always be rainbows and star dust" like in her romance novels.

When they adjourned to the living room Paul motioned Maria over to the Christmas tree. 'It's this one here.' he said, pointing to one of the bulbs on the string of fairy lights.

Frances, Charlie, Jason and Louis looked over expectantly.

Maria looked into the tree and tried to pull the faulty bulb out. 'There's something stuck on it I think.' she said, pulling at a piece of cotton that seemed to be tied around the base of the bulb. 'I think I have it.' and to her surprise, as she pulled up the cotton, out came a little box. 'Oh!' she said, holding a little, red-velvet box in her hand.

Frances, Charlie, Jason and Louis continued to look on, as Paul got down on one knee before Maria, cleared his throat, and said, 'My darling Maria. You are my everything. My reason to breathe and my reason to wake up. You have been with me through everything. We have raised two admirable children and we have worked hard together to build this beautiful family and home. I recognise that you have put so much effort in. You always do. You have always been there for all of us. And I know I don't tell you as often as I should, but, quite frankly, I don't think I can live in a world without you in it. Will you marry me?' and he smiled as he added, 'Again.'

Tears of joy ran down Maria's face and splashed onto the little, red-velvet box. With her hand over her mouth, Maria nodded vigorously, then removing her hand from her mouth said, 'Yes, yes of course I will.'

Paul stood up, and carefully opening the box in Maria's hand, he revealed a beautiful gold ring, with a large, green, emerald stone, flanked by two, white, pear-shaped diamonds.

Paul continued, 'I wish I could have bought you this when we first got engaged. I know it won't have the same sentimental attachment as your engagement ring, but I hope you like it just as much.' He took the ring from its box and placed it on the ring finger of Maria's right hand. It was a perfect fit.

Maria looked down at her hand, watching the ring twinkling in the Christmas tree lights. She knew that this Christmas was very, very special.

14. MATCHMAKERS

Emily closed the lid on her expensive laptop with a satisfying click and flopped back on the sofa. Her soft, brown waves falling about her shoulders as she did so.

Done. She felt . . . relieved. No, more than that . . . she felt free.

It was a scary step, but to be honest she was a rubbish accountant. She needed to do something that she felt passionate about, she needed to feel like she had made her mark on the world. She wanted to help people and give something back.

In her heart Emily was an old school romantic. She loved a happy ending, whether it was marriage and kids or companionship and kindred spirits. Emily couldn't help it. When she met people and talked to them for a little while, she just *knew* who their perfect fit would be. And she wasn't just being interfering.

Emily's female line of the family had a rather special and rather unusual talent: an instinctive romantic knowing. They were a female line of matchmakers. Emily's grandmother said that it was the Romany Gypsy blood in them.

When Emily was young, she watched with awe as young men and young women came to her grandmother for advice on love, or for little potions to increase their allure and enchant their beloved. Emily's mum also had the talent but she decided that she was happy to be a modern, New Age woman; she didn't need a man. Emily's mum rejected the romantic sixth sense that she had been born with. For Emily's fourteenth birthday her mum gifted Emily *The Female Eunuch* rather than encourage her romantic intuition.

As Emily matured into a young woman, she decided to follow a distinctly "normal", pedestrian, work existence; she became an accountant. It appeared that the matchmaker gift had ended with Emily's grandmother.

Then, when Emily hit thirty, something changed. She found her job increasingly boring and spent most of her workday daydreaming out of the window, mentally matching up her work colleagues and envisaging their first dates. Her weekends were spent watching *The Bachelor* or *The Bachelorette*. Emily found it hard to describe to her friends why she'd decided to quit her well paid job and set up a dating agency with her savings. In an affectionate way most of them thought she was crazy.

'You must be mad!' her best friend Jo teased her over drinks that weekend.

Beth piped up, 'Always the bridesmaid never the bride?' Emily winced at the jibe. It was true that love had eluded her. She was able to set up matches for others but never her own perfect match.

On one thing though they were all wrong. Because, as with most things in Emily's well-ordered life, her idea had been carefully thought out. She wasn't crazy.

The very next Monday morning, at nine sharp, Emily reopened her laptop and started work on her business plan for "Matchmakers – A Personalised Dating Service." Within a year Emily had hired a personal assistant. Her business, unsurprisingly, was a great success.

* * *

Emily's personal assistant, Rosalie, sat down with Emily and reviewed the appointments for the first week of December.

'We have three new clients to interview today.' she said, mentally ticking them off and looking her electronic organiser. 'Our first appointment is Dennis, an elderly gent. Looking for a replacement for his wife of fifty years.' Emily tilted her head sympathetically and thought, "Ah, the great loves never to be replaced."

Rosalie continued, 'Mark, in his late forties, a bit flash with his money. He keeps picking up gold-diggers, and gets stuck on looks, but *he says* he wants marriage and children.' "Hum," Emily thought. "He wants a clever, motherly wife but goes for pretty gold-diggers; there is a problem here."

Rosalie finished her list, 'And finally Nico, a businessman, very suave, tall and black.'

'And?' questioned Emily, waiting for Rosalie's interpretation. Rosalie was as organised as Emily; she was also interpersonally astute.

'Errr . . . well . . . and he wants a girlfriend?'

Emily raised an eyebrow at Rosalie. It was unusual that Rosalie hadn't got any more than that from the introductory video the clients were requested to upload.

Rosalie filled the silence with facts. 'Oh, and he's your last appointment of the day.'

'Ok. Good. Well let's get this day rolling.' Obviously, Emily would have to suss Nico out for herself.

* * *

Dennis was a well-presented gentleman. He wore a sports jacket which he appeared to have ironed. He'd also had a fresh haircut and smelt strongly of Old Spice aftershave. He was nervous.

Emily's heart went out to him. She got up from behind the desk, where she was interviewing him, and motioned for them to move to the sofas at the corner of her office.

Emily directed their interaction: 'If it's comfortable with you I believe we need to have an honest heart-to-heart. Would you like a tea or a coffee before we start?'

'Oh, thank you very much. Could I have a tea, white with sugar?'

'Of course.' Emily replied. As she brewed the tea, she noticed that he fidgeted and fussed. He obviously felt uncomfortable, but, he was brave enough to be here today. He was ready to make a change but he was scared.

Emily returned with the teas and sat next to him on the sofa. Gently she said, 'If it's comfortable with you, please tell me about your late wife.'

Dennis's eyes misted over and his face glowed as he recollected their beautiful marriage together. Two things became very apparent after he'd finished talking: he felt guilty for thinking of dating another woman and he was very lonely.

Emily took his hands in hers and said, 'I can tell from your description that you had a beautiful marriage. Your wife was loving and practical. Tell me, if you had died before her, do you think you would have wanted her lonely or would you have wished her to have companionship and friendship?'

Without hesitation Dennis agreed he would have done anything for her happiness.

Emily nodded, 'Well don't you think she feels the same. Watching you lonely must give her pain. She clearly loved and cared for you. You are not trying to replace her, but I don't think you are destined to be alone. It seems to me you have a kind heart and you have a lot of care to give. Have you considered there may be a lady out there in exactly the same situation as you?' The elderly man shook his head with the realisation that he hadn't, he'd been too engrossed in his own loneliness and loss.

Emily smiled at Dennis, as the realisation dawned on him that he didn't need to feel guilty for not wanting to be lonely. In fact, he could be doing someone a favour by offering them companionship too. His shoulders visibly rose and his face lifted. It was as if a weight had been removed from him.

Emily mentally ran through the ladies on her books. There were three that would suit him. But there was one who would be a great match. Emily had a good feeling about the pairing. This particular lady painted abstract art and liked walking her dog on the beach. Yes, something in her gut told her they would get on very well.

Smiling she said, 'Dennis, I have a lovely lady I'd like you to take out on a date. I'm going to give you her phone number. I will let her know you are going to call. I expect you to have set up a date with her in the next week. I will call you to see how things have gone. Does that sound ok?'

Dennis nodded slowly. It was strange to him that someone was suggesting a companion. But what had he got to lose?

* * *

Emily's second appointment of the day was a sharp contrast to Dennis.

Mark Fuller swaggered into Emily's office. As he approached her desk, he seemed to lead trousers first. From behind him in the doorway Rosalie raised an eyebrow before quietly closing the door.

Mark started to mark his territory by pulling out the chair and moving it at an angle. He dropped his Porsche car keys on the desk and with confidence, splayed back in the chair, his leather jacket creaking open as he did so, revealing his "aroma de armpit" and other items on display for Emily to admire.

Emily stared at him. He didn't impress her. Sadly, his attempts at confidence and masculinity were quite clearly superficial. He was covering up a broken heart from when he was young, she guessed. Until he worked his way through that pain he was destined to have superficial relationships and superficial women, as he would never be able to commit. Which was something, he said, he so desperately wanted to do.

Emily glanced at the photograph of her grandmother on her desk and internally rolled her eyes to her. She decided to test him.

'Good afternoon Mark. Would you like a tea or a coffee before we get started?'

'No thanks love, I've just come from my office and I've been drinking coffee in meetings all day.'

'Ok. Well, let's get started. Could you list me some of the qualities you are looking for in your ideal woman?'

Mark reeled off a list of qualities that only a

goddess could fulfil.

Emily summed up his requirements. 'I can only think of one woman I know who can fulfil such and impressive list.' Mark leant forward in anticipation, 'J-Lo.' Mark laughed with the release of tension. Emily didn't.

'Mr Fuller, you are wasting my time, the time of the ladies on my books and your own life unless we really get to the bottom of what is going on here.' Mark looked scared as she pulled down his walls. 'Who hurt you?' For the first time that afternoon Mark was mute. He gulped the air like a fish. 'Ok,' Emily continued, 'Let's start with your first proper relationship, shall we?'

'Well – ' Mark started as he grasped in the dark for something to say. Then he burst into tears. Emily dutifully passed him a tissue as she came round the desk.

Kneeling beside him, Emily patted him gently on the arm and said, 'I think it's time we got this sorted, don't you? If it really is a committed relationship with marriage and kids that you are looking for?'

Through his eyes full of tears and his snotty nose, Mark managed to nod.

* * *

Emily set Mark up with an initial appointment with a counsellor, and the promise that if he worked on his fear of commitment, he would be allowed to pick a date from one of three beautiful women she had in mind for him from her books. Set up with his carrot and stick, a slightly shaky Mark left her office on the road to love recovery.

Emily had half an hour before her last appointment of the day. She flicked through her Instagram, liking a few pictures of home interiors. As she admired the home décor, she wondered if she might have time to change out her settee before Christmas. She fancied a teal, velvet Chesterfield sofa. Something bold. Emily usually went for muted tones and a minimalist style, but her tastes had been changing; she found she was starting to like the idea of a unique, bold, quality piece.

As she scrolled through her feed an idea struck her. She didn't usually do this. But could it hurt? Just this once? She opened google and typed in "Nico Marksman". Google returned a very impressive LinkedIn page: Nico Marksman – Advertising Director and CEO of Marksman Marketing.

Emily put her phone down. She felt a little unsettled. This wasn't like her at all. Picking up her makeup bag she went to the bathroom and checked her appearance in the mirror. She reapplied her lipstick and wiped off the mascara smudge from under her eyes. Exiting the bathroom, she looked over to Rosalie working at her desk.

The entrance to Matchmakers was impressively

chic, decorated with pared-down creams, whites and greys. As it was the holiday season a pretty, white-lit tree, with a few silver baubles, sparked next to the light-grey, comfy sofas and a coffee table with assorted, current magazines on top.

Rosalie looked up from her desk. 'Nico has called to cancel.' she said.

'Oh!' Emily said in surprise.

'He said he was caught up in a family emergency. Something to do with his daughter.' Emily didn't know he had a daughter. Why did she know so little about this mysterious client? 'I've rearranged for Wednesday.' Rosalie finished.

'Ok, good. Rosalie, could you send me the link for Nico's bio video? I'd like to give it another review.'

'Sure.' Rosalie replied. She knew Emily wouldn't get any more out of it than she had. But it wasn't her place to ask why.

* * *

On Wednesday, at three p.m. sharp, there was a knock on Emily's office door.

'Come in!' Emily called out.

Rosalie opened the door and led in a very large man. Nico Marksman was at least six foot two, his skin was like dark chocolate, as were his big, kind eyes. He was smartly dressed in a crombie coat and scarf, to ward off the December cold. His clothes were muted shades of blue and grey, except for the most extraordinary pair of dark-red,

Italian, leather shoes. He gave off an air of calm confidence. Slowly he moved forward towards Emily's desk with a proffered hand and gentle smile.

Emily was like a motionless deer, stunned by the lights of an oncoming car. She couldn't move. She was completely helpless to prevent the crash.

Mustering as much self-awareness as she could, she managed to stand and extend her hand as they touched, "Hello." She was just conscious of Nico uttering apologies for missing his Monday appointment with her. She was aware of Rosalie looking a little oddly at her while she stood stupefied. Rosalie took the initiative and offered Nico a drink.

Emily's phone buzzed and broke the spell.

'I'm so sorry.' she said, coming to. 'How unprofessional!' With a smile she stowed her phone in her desk drawer. Rosalie came over with a black coffee and realising Emily was back on form, made her excuses and left.

'Once again,' Nico said, 'I'm so sorry about Monday. My daughter was ill at school and my ex-wife wasn't able to collect her.'

'Not at all!' Emily warmly replied. 'We all have personal lives.'

'Do you?' Nico asked frankly. He'd noticed Emily didn't have a ring on her left hand.

Emily blushed and hid her hand. 'I'm pretty sure we are here to discuss you.' she replied.

'Very well.' said Nico, and he sat there waiting for

the process to start.

Emily was completely blank. This had never happened to her before. She couldn't read him at all. Falling back to her routines, Emily went through the motions of taking out her notebook and fountain pen, as she asked some stock questions. But ten minutes later she was still none the wiser. Feeling completely off guard she decided to hold a mixer party for him. Perhaps Rosalie would help her select some potential matches. She really wished she'd asked Rosalie to stay for this interview.

'Well, Nico,' Emily said, as she impressively finished writing meaningless words in her notebook. 'I think the best initial course of action is to hold a mixer party for you. This is where we invite ten potential matches and you get to choose one for a first date. How does that sound?'

Nico looked deeply into her eyes as he replied, 'You're the love expert. That sounds fine to me.'

'Wonderful. Well, let's put something in the diary. How about Friday the twelfth of December? Let's get things started before everyone is off for the holidays.'

He looked at her intently as he replied, 'That sounds perfect. I have a question though.'

'Of course.'

'Will you be there?'

Electricity passed up Emily's spine as she tried to remain composed. 'Absolutely Nico, this is specialist matchmaking service. Rosalie and I will of course be in attendance to make sure everything goes to perfection.'

He smiled and repeated her last word back to her, 'Perfection. *Mmm*. Well, thank you very much Emily. I have every confidence you are going to find me my perfect match.' Nico politely shook her hand, as she got up to show him out.

* * *

Emily stood looking blankly at her wardrobe. It was the night of the mixer for Nico, and she had half an hour before she needed to be back out the door again.

She let her hand reach up and touch some of her favourite dresses. Blue silk? No too sexy. Red bodycon? No, way too sexy, she was supposed to be making the matches not competing with them. Her hand moved along. Little black dress? Yes, a little black dress would be perfect, professional yet still in keeping with the vibe of the mixer event.

Emily surveyed herself in the mirror. The dress was a structured, black, asymmetric in style, with pleats running from the shoulder and wrapping the waist. She teamed this with classic, black-leather stilettoes and a neat matching black-leather clutch. Her hair was styled in her signature big, brown waves. Emily added her gold hoop earrings and a chunky, gold watch. Finally, she added a swipe of bright red lipstick to complete the look. She looked perfect; she felt petrified. What if tonight wasn't a success? What if she failed?

Rosalie was already at the hotel venue. She was so efficient that there was little left for Emily to do, other than meet the ladies as they arrived for the mixer party. In truth Emily had struggled to select the ladies, so Rosalie had suggested they have a mixture of personalities and hopefully someone would stick. Emily felt nervous, this hadn't happened to her before. She always *knew* who would match. Her gift had never failed her up until she met Nico.

By the time Nico arrived the ladies were happily sipping cocktails in the hotel's function room, waiting for him. Emily greeted him in the hotel lobby. As she walked towards him, she watched his eyes appraise her. She felt very visible in what she thought would be a dress to meld into the background.

'Nico!' she smiled warmly, offering her hand.

Nico gently took her smaller hand in his massive one. His Rolex shook under the grey, cashmere sleeve of his overcoat.

'Wonderful to see you again Emily.'

'Ready for your mixer?'

Smiling at her he replied, 'Show me the way.'

The mixer was a great success. With Nico's warm, gentle manner, impressive height, and obvious wealth, he was a catch. The ladies buzzed around him like bees to a honey pot. Rosalie just about managed to prise him away to a separate room, to privately discuss with Emily who he would like to take on a first date.

Nico was still smiling and buzzing from the attention when Rosalie directed him to the table where Emily was sitting. Rosalie joined them and opened her electronic organiser.

'How did it go?' Emily asked. 'Did you find a lady this evening that you'd like to take on a first date?'

Nico replied confidently, 'Yes I have.'

'Wonderful! Who is it?' said Emily.

'You.' replied Nico.

Rosalie efficiently checked through Emily's planner as she replied, 'Emily has a spare slot next Tuesday evening for a first date.'

Emily sat open mouthed.

'Perfect.' said Nico, and turning to Emily said, 'I look forward to it.'

All Emily's brain could cobble together was, 'Thank you.'

Rosalie closed her organiser with a satisfactory snap. If you looked closely, it was barely perceptible, you could see a little smile at the edge of her mouth. Rosalie was very good at her job.

Emily turned to her personal assistant and trusted friend as Nico left the hotel. 'He picked me?' she said. Although Emily wouldn't admit it, Beth's jibe of, "Always the bridesmaid – " still sat deep in her heart.

Rosalie allowed herself to smile at her boss and friend. 'Yes Emily, he picked you. And don't forget the one-drink rule on the first date . . . Shall I go and give the news to the ladies next door?'

Emily thought of all those beautiful ladies, and that out of all of them he'd picked her. All her professionalism left her. 'Would you?' she said, relieved. How could she face them now?

'Of course. You need to prepare for you date next Tuesday!'

* * *

Emily was back at her wardrobe, but this time Rosalie sat on her bed directing her. Rosalie flicked through Emily's copy of *The Female Eunuch* which sat on her bedside table.

'Yes,' Rosalie said as Emily's hand hovered, 'the red one.'

Emily got changed in the bathroom and came back for Rosalie's inspection.

'Perfect.' Rosalie said. 'And with your signature red lipstick I think Nico will be blown away.'

Emily laughed over her embarrassment. Blown away by her? It seemed such a bizarre concept. She still couldn't get over the fact that he'd picked her. Yes, she knew there was chemistry. But it seemed strange that the matchmaker got matched. And she didn't see it coming.

Appraising herself in the mirror Emily said to Rosalie, 'Did you see the match?'

'Yes.' Rosalie said candidly. 'Right, best get on or you'll be late.'

* * *

Rosalie dropped Emily off at the restaurant. The restaurant had a smart, black, glossy sign over the window and was lit by brass downlighters, flanked by green draping plants and seasonally surrounded by racing, white, Christmas lights.

Nico stood at the door waiting for her, with flowers and a little present. As she walked up to him, he lightly wrapped his arm around her waist and kissed her cheek. It was as if electricity buzzed through her spine. Her cheeks flushed red to match her dress and her lipstick.

'Shall we go in?' he directed.

'Yes.' She held his hand as he led her inside.

The evening was perfect. They talked without pause. They laughed and enjoyed each other's company. It was a cold December night outside, but inside the restaurant it was warm and the atmosphere twinkled with sparkles.

Nico paid the bill and helped Emily put on her coat Emily picked up her flowers as they headed for the door, as she did so she realised she hadn't opened her present.

'Oh!' she said in embarrassment. 'I forgot to open my gift!'

Nico held the restaurant door open for her and laughed with a deep, smooth rumble. 'Keep it for home if you like.'

'Oh no! I must open it now.'

In the light of the restaurant lamps she slid her manicured nails under the wrapping paper. Inside was a box of Matchmakers chocolates – *cool mint.*

Immediately she laughed. 'I see! Matchmakers! Very funny.'

Nico winked at her. 'Did it escape your attention the matchmaker got matched?'

'Do you know, you are the only person I've ever met that I couldn't match. I just didn't have any instinct for who you would match with, because, I guess it was me.'

Nico smiled as he replied, 'I'm in advertising. I'd seen you in a bar the week before I'd called for an appointment. I knew that the best way to get you to notice me was to advertise myself to you. What better way than become your client?' Nico gently took her hand as he pulled her towards him. 'I'm assuming that this is going to be something that we can continue?'

Even in her heels Emily was still much shorter than Nico. Looking up at him she nodded her affirmation as he stooped down to kiss her. His soft lips meeting hers for the first time.

Above them the Christmas lights raced, as Emily held the box of matchmakers tightly in her hand.

THE END

Thank you for reading:

The Adventure of the Christmas Cracker
and other short stories

I would be so grateful if you would give

me a review. Happy Christmas! HL x

Printed in Great Britain
by Amazon

18791879R00129